# Mr. Pettigrew

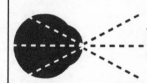

This Large Print Book carries the
Seal of Approval of N.A.V.H.

THE NEMESIS SERIES, BOOK 3

# MR. PETTIGREW

## L. J. MARTIN

**WHEELER PUBLISHING**
A part of Gale, a Cengage Company

**GALE**
A Cengage Company

Farmington Hills, Mich • San Francisco • New York • Waterville, Maine
Meriden, Conn • Mason, Ohio • Chicago

GALE
A Cengage Company

Copyright © 2012 by L. J. Martin.
A Nemesis Series Novel.
Wheeler Publishing, a part of Gale, a Cengage Company.

**LIBRARY OF CONGRESS CIP DATA ON FILE.**
**CATALOGUING IN PUBLICATION FOR THIS BOOK**
**IS AVAILABLE FROM THE LIBRARY OF CONGRESS**

ISBN-13: 978-1-4328-6215-2 (softcover)

Published in 2019 by arrangement with L. J. Martin

Printed in Mexico
1 2 3 4 5 6 7 23 22 21 20 19

# MR. PETTIGREW

# CHAPTER ONE

Now, even the thought of food turns my stomach.

Fact is it's becoming alien to that organ, as unwelcome as a poxed and profane whore teaching Sunday school.

And I'm beginning to wonder if I really give a tinker's damn; such are the mental machinations of the physical act of starving to death.

But rather than merely lay down and die, which I have an inclination to do, I go ahead and make the hard dismount from the revolting stench of the empty cattle car onto the razor-edged rocks of the rail bed, and, as usual, fall in the process, pitching forward, skinning the heels of both hands so blood seeps from the abrasions — a pile of rocks being no place for a peg to find purchase. It's a long row to hoe just getting back upright on foot and stump, and I struggle, but do so. Not without muttering a curse or two.

It's been a year since a Union cannon ball took, and a carpenter clumsily replaced, my extremity, and I'm still not totally conversant with the needs of operating a peg. Particularly one that's not totally settled itself onto one's stub. A good part of that year was spent in the healing then hobbling about on crutches — and cursing.

Were I a man of means I'd have a decent prosthetic constructed, one upon which I could place a boot or brogan and fool folks into thinking me whole, if gimpy. I have seen some advertisements from the American Limb Company, which would give some hope, were I not destitute.

The hell of it is, we discovered the war had officially ended two days before that cursed cannon was fired and we, and the bluecoats across the mile-wide meadow, remained ignorant of Appomattox as the wire that would have brought us word in the form of Morse code, had been cut by our own gray coat. Damn the blue tail flies, and the lousy luck. Good luck kept me alive, good luck did not keep me whole. I occasionally curse my good luck.

When finally the task of disembarking my royal coach is accomplished, I eye the town, which seems to be coming alive as the sun's last rays retreat in the wake of a torrid day.

For the last four hours I've stayed hidden, partially covered in odorous bedding straw, not wanting a railroad bull to bust my head . . . but then began to wonder if a crushed skull wasn't a better way to go than starving. A pick handle up aside the noggin would seem to end things with some sweet suddenness, whereas starving seems a long drawn out unpleasant affair.

However there's light and the sounds of libations and frivolity coming from an establishment only a couple of hundred gimpy paces ahead. Its glimmering windows give one the slightest smidgeon of hope. And providence has delivered me to this town, which I believe, if I've judged the distance correctly, is called Nemesis. There was no conductor calling out the stops.

Like most on the Transcontinental Line, except the Bucket of Blood up the line, the Angel Cloud Saloon, upon which I'm gazing, most likely belies its name. Unless of course the cloud refers to the cigar and roll-your-own smoke that most likely hangs from the rafters to waist high before each night is over. I am damn sure there'll be no angels in attendance, no matter what the name implies, unless the soiled variety counts as such. Or possibly the angels seen alternatively with the devils, wafting about the ceiling amidst the smoke, by the opium users in the den below. All this I conclude as there's a descending stairway on the side of the saloon, with a sign in both Chinese characters and English, announcing "Heavenly Retreat."

The boardwalk is a high one — knee high to a tall mule — and I have my dollop of trouble mounting it to take a peek into the batwing doors, as the peg I'd been fitted with still chafes my stump badly and I have to keep its taper securely planted in the mud in order to hoist my good left leg up while hanging onto one of the six by six posts supporting the Cloud's porch roof. I can only barely hide the wince it causes, and my brows seem now already permanently creased with the incessancy of its pain. I fear it's making me old and furrowed before my time.

Most of the hell on wheels towns that sprang up along the Transcontinental are long dead and gone, but Nemesis has prevailed — as was passed along to me up the line by another taking advantage of free, but risky, transportation on the road — due to some nearby mines and a muddy river that waters some sparse valleys which in turn feed stock on a half dozen hard scrabble hand-to-mouth ranches.

The cold desert night — in contrast to the simmering day just departed — is racking my backbone with shudders which are now working their way up to rattle my teeth; bone chilling cold but with as many stars as grains of sand in the nearby desert laughing down at we lowly mortals. The desert is as beautiful, and as fickle, as any woman I've met . . . some of whom had as many thorns.

When I was two-legged, I met my share of the fairer sex, in fact had the reputation of being somewhat the Lothario in Charleston, the last real town I frequented before Fort Sumter fell to the Confederacy, which in turn turned it into the primary target of many a northern general and Union gun boat. With the subsequent threat to my family's plantation, I rebelled and joined the cause.

Even though I am down to a lousy dime and a nickel — one beer and a fistful of soda crackers — I'm thinking I can get lost in a crowded saloon and take advantage of the warmth from a cast-iron stove, and the rancid body heat of four or five dozen townsmen, drovers, and drummers, all trying to relieve the house of faro and roulette money. Warm air, but flavored with the acrid odor of hard working men, only a few of whom color bath water on a weekly basis, all of whom whose odor is only somewhat tempered with the lilac water splashed on a pair of soiled doves who are wafting about like moths lured by the flicker of silver lining men's pockets. How-some-ever, the ability to relieve these establishments of money normally meant one was only better at bottom dealing, the punishment for which in lawless towns such as Nemesis is the removal of a thumb the first time, and your head if caught again. And there are normally plenty of Bowie knifes nearby to accomplish the tasks.

Winning, I learned long ago, is a feat seldom accomplished on tables and decks rigged for the house.

With luck, they'll have a hog's head barrel of goobers free to the customers. A couple of handfuls of those will keep me going for another day or so, if I can sidle up to it before I'm recognized as a bindle stiff. Of course as my coat becomes more and more threadbare and pasture patty smeared, that task is less of a chore. I'll likely not be mistaken for a prosperous banker or cattle baron.

Finally managing to get my left boot hoisted up on the boardwalk, I pull myself up and free the peg from the mud with a popping suck like the freedom of a champagne cork. The sound brings back fond memories and some encouragement.

I get upright and whack my peg on the road side edge of the worn boardwalk a few times to free it of a gob of wet desert, then head for the batwings.

Just as I reach out to push them open, they fly in my face, and they and a man a half a head taller than myself crashes into me, knocking me windless and air-borne back off the boardwalk into the mud. I flop to my belly and have to scramble to keep out from under the hoofs of a pair of saddled mounts tied there, when some big fellow flies off the boardwalk and lands flush on me, driving my face down into the mud. I come up spitting and choking, and hearing the laughter of men gathering on the boardwalk, mingled with that of the horses jerking free and whinnying as they pound away.

Had the derringer in my tattered waistcoat pocket been loaded, I'd have jerked it.

# CHAPTER TWO

Spitting and snorting I get the crud cleared out of my eyes and hack my mouth clean, only then to see an extended hand. Reaching for it, I grasp a claw grizzled and scarred, and he pulls me upright with surprising ease. I'm not a big man, but of average weight, even shy of a leg just below the knee, and sucking me out of that mud and totally upright with an easy stroke requires a man of some strength.

He is not smiling, not that it would be easy to surmise as he sports a thick mustache, nicely waxed and curled upward, but rather is looking over my shoulder like a bull studying a bastard calf. His hair is more black than gray, but his mustache more gray, or even white, than black. Were I inclined to admire men, I'd say him handsome in a stately sort of way.

I hear commotion behind me and turn to see the big man who'd knocked me flying,

14

disappearing, chunks of mud flying from his boots as he runs. He picks them up and puts them down with purpose, like a hungry wolf after a wounded moose already dragging a gut. I turn back and only then notice the sawed off scattergun hanging loosely in Mr. Mustache's left hand. Even in the dim light flowing out of the saloon I can see blood covering the butt-end of the ugly weapon. It is surely a weapon for close work, its stock cut down to a pistol grip and its barrels to no more than twelve inches, but it seems it's been used as a bludgeon.

His voice is low and raspy, as if he's just come in from a month in a blizzard. "Sorry you got in the middle of that, stranger. Hard to keep your balance with that peg."

Pity is never a thing I look for in another man — in fact the thought of it sours my gullet. But somehow I sense that it isn't pity this man is offering. I won't say he has kind eyes, but they sure aren't condemning or judgmental.

"Damned if it ain't, at times," I offer. "But it comes in real handy if you and your'n are planting corn or pumpkins or such."

"I can see how it would," he comes close to a tight smile, but not quite, and some of the men on the boardwalk laugh out loud.

He continues, "My business is done inside, but I'd be proud if you'd come on in and let me stand you to a steak, beans, and a draught of suds. You look a mite like a fella what's been lost in the desert for a month or more."

I feel my face color a bit. "I'm a mite lost, all right. Don't have a way to repay you, Mister . . . Mister?" I extend my hand again.

"Pettigrew," he says.

"Mr. Pettigrew."

"Don't expect to be repaid, Mister . . . Mister?" In another man I might think him mocking me, but he's got a gleam in his eye that hints at humor, not scorn. He gives me that almost-smile again.

So I speak up, and truthfully. "Boone. Beau Banquo Boone. I'm a traveling man, recently housed in the cattle car hotel over on the Transcontinental. Traveling subtourist class, as you might surmise."

"Banquo?"

"Named for the good general in MacBeth. My father was a follower of the play write."

"It seems your father was also partial to the letter 'b.' So you could use that steak?"

"I could, Mr. Pettigrew, but first I'd like to know to what I owe this kindness?"

"Why, I knocked ol' Rosco Wilkenson out those swinging doors and caused you to get

16

your first course of Nemesis hospitality as a mouthful of piss-mud and horseshit. I figure that's enough reason."

"So you're the official town greeter?" I can see by the look and the lack of an answer that I'm pushing my luck, and a steak and beans would be luck indeed. So I quickly add, "I'm Beau, if you don't mind the familiarity. You got a first name, Mr. Pettigrew?"

"It'll be A. Pettigrew on my headstone. But Pettigrew will do."

"Then Mr. Pettigrew it will be. I'm obliged. And I hope your headstone and epitaph are in the far distant future."

The men on the boardwalk, most of their hands holding chips they've snatched up from tables inside, laugh again then begin filtering back into the saloon.

The place is typical of here-today-gone-tomorrow railroad towns: clapboard walls, a fine Brunswick back-bar, but one that can be taken apart to transport; and a solid maple fore bar as well, but it, too, can be separated into three ten foot segments for transport. Whom-so-ever built the place did so with move-on-soon in mind. Nine tables down the middle of the saloon lay between the bar and two faro tables which flank a centered roulette table and wheel along the far wall from the bar, all again surrounded by raucous men as they return to prior endeavors. Goober peanut shells cover the floor, not nearly so interesting now that a steak is promised. Towels hang at five-foot intervals under the bar, and a dozen nicely polished brass spittoons are scattered about. The obligatory image of a reclining scantily clad lady of rather generous proportions looks down seductively from her perch high in the center of the back bar. The kitchen is likely out back, a few steps from the back door, to reduce the chance of fire, and the privy a few steps beyond. Since it's not a two story structure I presume there are also cribs out back for the use of the soiled doves.

Nothing unique about the place, at least not so as one would notice.

Mr. Pettigrew, nicely dressed I can't help but admire, with striped trousers, a four in hand tie, brocade waistcoat with some fancy needle work and turtle shell buttons, gold watchchain and fob with a pearl the size of a 44 caliber slug on its end and I presume a gold watch on the other. And that mustache, perfectly trimmed and waxed.

Mr. Pettigrew is not much for conversation, as we sit and sip our suds without talking until my grub arrives — I succumb to his silence after asking if he is sitting shotgun in the saloon, and get a rough look and no answer. Obviously he considers the suggestion a slight. He's a man who seems to find a slight in much that's said.

The smell of steak, fried taters, and beans quickly belies my belief that a bite of vittles would offend, and I reach for the knife and fork as quickly as they land in front of me. However, my stomach's been flapping against my backbone for so long I'm a bit concerned with its attitude toward a red meat invasion.

After I get a couple of bites down — my stomach churning and fluttering as if a couple of belfry bats have invaded rather than red meat — he finally speaks up. "So, you got business in Nemesis?"

"No, sir. Not unless someone's got work for a one legged artilleryman. Are you the law hereabouts, Mr. Pettigrew?"

"Nope."

That, too, seems to offend. I notice he has a habit of smoothing his mustache when irritated. Were I a gambling man, I'd call that a tell, and even not being I'll watch out for it.

But he continues, "That was a personal matter, an offence in a game of cards, you got into the middle of." His gaze drifts over the room, a sign of a careful man verifying the safety of his surroundings, then he continues, "So, what skills do you possess, Mr. Boone?"

"Well, sir, I can drop a cannon shell inside a fifty foot circle at damn nigh a mile. Other than that, not much."

"Not much demand for artillerymen hereabouts, now that the recent unpleasantries are concluded," Mr. Pettigrew says, and I get that almost smile again. "Anything else?"

The use of the term, recent unpleasantries leads me to believe he was a butternut man, and no damn Yankee, but I refrain from asking, and rather suggest, "You didn't ask for which side?"

"Don't matter to me, Mr. Boone, and it's time it stopped mattering to the rest of the country."

"I agree."

"Then if you agree, that probably means you fought for the gray?"

"Thought it didn't matter?"

"It don't. So what skills might you have?"

"I was a cowpoke in the yards back in Omaha, last paying job I had. Back home in South Carolina, when we had a home, I watched over lots of . . . of employees . . . who worked the fields, growing cotton and

20

a little rice."

"So, no more slaves to oversee?"

I ignore the question. "But the corrals I see out there on the edge of town don't look to be busy enough to support no cowpokes, nor do I notice any fields of rice hereabouts in need of an horticultural expert."

"No fields of any kind, other than meadow grass, and it tends itself. And the corrals . . . only once't a year at round-up time. What else?"

"I was a swamper before I took up cowpokin'. And I've worked the bar some."

"Hold on," he gets up and disappears into the back of the place, from where a greasy Chinaman had appeared with the steak I am busy polishing off. It is the first real food I've had in four days, and for a moment my gut feels as if it houses a ball of cottonmouths; I am afraid I soon won't be able to keep it down if the serpents don't stop their wiggling. I sit quiet for a few moments, until I am forced to teeter up on foot and peg, as Mr. Pettigrew reappears with a square jawed but attractive woman at his side, a woman with cat yellow eyes and rouge reddened lips who looks as if she could see straight though a body, right into his very soul. Her crimson faille dress is trimmed in lace, and, with only a slight bodice, has the cut somewhere between a soiled dove and a Christian spinster lady . . . hard to judge.

"Alice, this is Mr. Boone. A new friend of mine."

I jerk off the floppy brimmed hat I'd managed to hang onto even after my tumble from the train car and dive into the mud under the saddle mounts, and nod, "Ma'am."

To my surprise, she extends her long fingered hand, her fingernails colored with some concoction, her grip firm but soft. It's a hand that's never pulled turnips or dug potatoes, more inclined, I imagine, to snipping roses.

"Nice to meet you, Mr. Boone," her smile seems genuine. "Any friend of Pettigrew's is a friend of mine. He tells me you might be seeking a position, and have some experience in establishments of this sort?"

"That's true, if you can call drawing a beer and swamping experience. I'm a little more than fair with numbers, should that be of service."

"I do my own money arrangements, however, I can pay you a dollar a day, all the beans you can eat . . . on your own time . . . and a mug or two of beer after hours. That wooden appendage won't keep you from giving a body an honest day's work, or emptying a spittoon when necessary?"

I lift my head a little higher, at the risk of seeming haughty. "Fact is, ma'am, it makes a body want to do a bit more than normally required."

She studies me a moment looking more than satisfied with that answer, nods, says, "fine then," and I'm shocked to realize that my eyes are filling with water. I have not shed a tear since a cougar et my dog when I was eight years old. I backhand my eyes with considerable self-consciousness.

Being a woman of some class she ignores that weakness and she says as she begins to move away, "Start in the morning, after breakfast, which employees take in the cook shed out back, a lick and a whistle after sun-up. In fact, you can sleep out in the kitchen should you need a place until you get on your feet." That embarrasses her a little as she realizes she might should have said foot. But she continues, "Cook stove keeps it warm a good while. Stay out of the pie safe unless you have a dime to leave in place of a piece. It's the building with the brick stack between here and the cribs." She waves over her shoulder, and is gone.

I extend my hand to Mr. Pettigrew, and catch a breath before I speak. It's all I can do to keep my voice from breaking. "Thank you, sir."

He ignores the hand and walks to a corner and snatches a fine wide-brimmed light colored beaver hat off a peg, settles it on his head and starts back my way, when I hear the batwings slam open.

"You son-of-a-bitch," echoes from the same large fellow I'd seen running away. Only this time he is charging forward, Winchester in hand, swinging it up, working the lever in the same motion.

It appears Mr. Pettigrew's epitaph may be imminent.

I'm between them, and for the second time tonight I take a dive. I hit the floor among the goober shells when the room reverberates with both the roar of a Winchester and a double barrel scattergun.

The place goes silent, except for the fellow who'd busted in bouncing off the front wall of the place, then crashing across my good leg. I try to see if Mr. Pettigrew has been hit, but the table and my dinner are knocked to the floor, blocking my view. It rolls aside, and there stands Mr. Pettigrew, the scattergun hanging loosely at his side, dust motes floating down from the rafters intermingling with black-powder smoke rising. The room, smelly as a battlefield, is now as silent as a tomb, as it seems every occupant holds their breath.

Then Mr. Pettigrew breaks the silence. "You all right, Mr. Boone?" he asks me in a low tone.

I pat myself down, not sure. "Yes, sir, I believe I am."

"Fine." He turns to the man on the floor, whose center section is a quivering mass of red mush. His voice low, Pettigrew shakes his head as he speaks. "It's a damn fool who goes up against two ounces of cut up square nails in a sawed down twelve gauge at a distance of only fifteen feet." Then he turns his attention back to me. "You sure you didn't get creased?"

I'm pleased I'm not holed, and smile at Mr. Pettigrew. "Damn sure." I clear my throat, glancing at the man still across my leg. "It seems your personal matter with this gentleman is concluded. Might we get him off'n me?"

He ignores my dark humor. "Fine, I'd hate to see you further injured. That was a fine piece of dive-for-cover you executed. So, you being okay let's get this holligan off'n your legs, . . . err, leg, and get you another steak. Seems we used what was left of yours to mop up the floor."

"Obliged," I manage, as he jerks the man aside then again drags me to foot and peg.

Some of the large gentleman follows, stuck to my already soiled trousers. It's a good thing I'm accustomed to gore and the smell of a man turned almost inside out. With the lead that's been flying over and around me, it's a better thing I haven't soiled my own trousers.

It's seldom one gets accustomed to cut up nails cutting the air like hornets near one's person.

# CHAPTER THREE

Sipping my beer for a good long while, I get the feel of the place before I retire to my assigned living quarters.

I'd constructed a pallet of some soiled table linens piled in a corner of the kitchen and awoke to my surprise to a bitterly cold morning, me attired skimpily and embarrassingly in tattered long johns, and, to my great chagrin, my clothes gone missing. What kind of a heartless beggar would steal a one-legged man's clothes while he slept in what would soon be a semi-public place?

By the time I manage to sit up, as I predicted, a rather rotund but rosy-cheeked woman waddles into the kitchen carrying an armload of wood, my privacy lost.

"Good mornin'," she says, seemingly unperturbed by a half-naked man. "Does Miss Alice know you're cluttering up my kitchen?"

"Ma'am," I sputter, "she told me to sleep

here. I'm here at her instruction. You'll please pardon my indiscretions. It seems someone has absconded with my attire."

"That would be Mr. Lum Sing Ho, doing Miss Alice's bidding. He'll return them long before I have to throw you out for being in my way. And you'll appreciate his wife's skill with a pot of water, a bar of lye soap, a flat iron, and a needle if necessary. In the meantime, if you'll stoke the fire up, I'll get a pot of coffee underway and you may enjoy a cuppa. I'm Penellope Jane, formerly of Manassas, Virginia. You can call me Penellope Jane, just plain Penny, or ma'am . . . suit yourself."

"My pleasure, Penellope Jane," I say, with a little more than a smidgen of embarrassment as my hairy butt cheeks are showing through a pair of indiscreetly placed holes worn in the flap of my undies. She is kind enough not to be obvious in her observance, and I'm modest enough to keep my back to the wall until she leaves the outbuilding, which she does promptly. My two-thirds leg is well covered as the long john has come unpinned and is flapping as I hop about, having not yet attended to it nor strapped on my peg.

By the time I have the fire stoked, a Chinaman, long braided queue hanging to his waist, whose height is less than my arm pit, appears at the doorway; his grin as constant as his bows. His lips are smiling, but his gaze intent, obsidian black eyes measuring everything in the room in an instant.

"Missy Awice have me do you duds."

"I'll have to owe you, Mr. Ho," I say, taking the bundle he offers.

"She do. Bye bye," he says, and is gone.

I hardly recognize my trousers, shirt, and waistcoat, as the tears are mended and patched, the buttons replaced, and all smells fresh as a Spring morning. I almost hate to place them on my not-so-fresh body, but modesty dictates. All but my hat and brogan is pressed flat as a salt-plain out on the desert we've just traversed. Even my wide brimmed hat has been brushed and re-shaped, and my brogan has been shined and the lace replaced — I wonder if he'll accept half-payment for the shoeshine, as it's a single shoe?

Speaking of halves, damned if I won't look half human, I decide, quickly donning the clothes before Miss Penellope Jane returns. Of course, I'm no longer much more than half a human, so looking it seems to make good sense. I almost wish I had a looking glass so I could admire myself.

I have my pant leg hoisted up and am trying to fit the peg in place when Miss Penellope Jane returns, carrying a bucket of water, I presume for the promised coffee. I'm happy to note that my job is well accomplished, as the cast iron stove is roaring.

It seems I'll never get over my reticence at having folks see my bare, reddened, bulbous, stub . . . which Miss Penellope Jane promptly notices as I try and fit the peg in place.

She takes on a grandmotherly demeanor. "That looks a mite tender. I have a can of bacon grease here if you'd like to give it a rub?"

"That's kind of you, ma'am, but I believe I'll just let it toughen up on its own."

"Suit yourself. Miss Alice is inside and wants a word with you."

Worrying that I should have already been at work with mop and bucket, I head out of the little kitchen shack and highball it for the saloon, as quickly as my stub, not yet quite settled, will allow.

Miss Alice is seated at a round table, this time in a yellow dress, pince-nez glasses perched on her delicate nose, going over a ledger book as I hobble up.

"Sit," she says, motioning to a chair across the table from her, without looking up.

I do, and wait patiently. The bartender, the same one who I'd noticed working the bar last night, wanders over and plants a mug in front of me then pours steaming coffee, black as a foot up a bull's butt.

"Obliged," I say, and he sticks out a long bony hand.

"I'm Horace Goodfellow," he says and I give him a shake.

"Beau Boone. Thanks for the mud."

The coffee is well cooled by the time Miss Alice looks up. "You sleep well."

"Yes, ma'am. Better than rocking along in a cattle car, soaking up what the steers leave behind."

"I imagine. I see you have clean clothes. Mr. Lo and his wife also keep a tent with a hot bath for rent. Draw two dollars from Mr. Goodfellow at the bar and go get yourself a hot bath and a shave, and whatever else you need from Trader Jake's General Store. Buy yourself some sweets and maybe we can get some meat on those bones." She removes a gold pocket watch from her reticule and checks the time. "They'll be open by the time you finish your bath, then get your shave and trim. Be here ready to go to work by nine thirty. The two will come out of your first pay."

"Yes, ma'am." I gulp my coffee down.

31

"You met Miss Penellope?"

"Yes, ma'am. A kind lady. I hope I didn't offend her as I was still in long johns when she reported for work."

"She nursed in the war, and raised a half dozen brothers, her being the oldest. Her mama and daddy were killed by a stray shell at Bull Run, and four of her bothers died in the war. She'll be a bit hard to offend, as will I. She'll have a batch of biscuits and a jug of honey out back if you return a little early."

"Yes, ma'am." I rise and start to head for the bartender, but she stops me short with a pointed question.

"You ever kill a man, Mr. Boone?"

I pause and weigh that unexpected, and somewhat surprising, question a moment before answering, then decide to answer truthfully. "More than I'd care to count, ma'am. I was, after all, over four years in the recent war. I carry four holes in my hide and still carry one ball in my back from them returning the favor from the other side of the affair."

"I don't imagine that makes it any easier killing the next one." She gives me a weary smile. "The reason I ask is I need an unknown to sit shotgun upon occasion. It is sometimes beneficial to have someone

32

unknown to the general population in such a job, as we all fear the unknown. It seems, as I've just learned, the gentleman I had on the job, one Cyrus Gibbs, absorbed an Arkansas toothpick in his gullet last night, over at Maddie's Pleasure Parlor, and will not be back to collect his week's pay. Rather than collect pay, he paid the wages of sin. Would you consider helping out if need be?"

"I don't relish the thought of blowing a man in half; only if need be dire, and should the pay be proper. I have no compunction against the necessary, so long as it's within the law."

"Your cadaverous appearance would frighten all but the most callous of men. Go get your bath and I'll discuss it with Pet."

"Pet?"

"Mr. Pettigrew, but don't take up the nickname. He hates even me calling him Pet."

"Oh, is Mr. Pettigrew your partner?"

"Only a trusted friend, but he'll be concerned with whomsoever fills the position. It seems he stirred the hornet's nest last evening."

"How so?"

"The fella he cut in half has four brothers. His father, Caleb Wilkenson, is the owner of a very successful mine with a half-dozen gunmen on the payroll to protect his product . . . gold . . . and another two dozen miners who seem ready to do the boss's bidding. Mr. Wilkenson with take considerable umbrage at losing a son."

"Sounds troubling. Will Mr. Pettigrew be leaving town?"

"Ha! You don't know Mr. Pettigrew. Go scrub the top layer off and top it all with a little lilac water to quell the smell of those road apples."

It's funny how the beneficent Lord keeps a fellow from smelling his own odors when he's been sans bathing for a good long while. But I manage a tight smile.

"Yes, ma'am."

As fate would have it, after I'd paid Mr. Ho a dime for the use of his copper tub, hot water, and bar of strong lye soap, Mr. Pettigrew is in the middle of a shave when I find the barber shop. As soon as I pass under the striped pole, and pull the door open, I get a chill down my back. As I only then realize Mr. Pettigrew's been tracking my progress past the window and into the door with a revolver, the barrel of which is only visible as a protruding lump under the blue cloth draped over him. His face is slathered with shaving soap, and the brindle headed barber is stropping his razor as I enter.

Mr. Pettigrew nods and seems to noticeably relax when he recognizes me, and the barrel sinks back so as to be not such a threatening lump.

"Mr. Pettigrew," I say, with a little extra politeness, snatching the hat from my head.

"Mr. Boone. Miss Alice give you the boot so soon?"

"No, sir. She suggested I get a bath and a shave, which I'm sure you know I badly needed, and was kind enough to provide me with an advance."

"Have a seat. There's a Leslie's Weekly there, only a couple of weeks old."

I take a ladder-back chair, and pick up the paper, only to ask, "You seem to be expecting trouble, if that lump is the hog-leg I expect it might be?"

"Mr. Boone, this is Andy McBride, a fine barber." It seems Mr. Pettigrew ignores my question, which I've noticed is a habit of his. I notice that barber McBride has a nice new Henry Model 1870 leaning in the corner, only a couple of steps from his tonsorial chair. So far, most of Nemesis seems to stay situated near a firearm. Doesn't speak well for the friendliness of the place.

I rise and cross the room to shake the redheaded barber's hand. His freckle face carries a wide grin, only missing one front tooth. He has to wipe the shaving soap away from his hands, which he uses to wipe the razor clean, but does so and follows with an honest shake, smile and nod, and I retake my seat.

"Mr. Boone," Pettigrew asks, "I'd appreciate it if you'd keep an eye out and tell me if anyone approaches. I'd like to catch a little shuteye while Andy finishes up."

"My pleasure. Women and children excluded I presume."

"Women and children excluded."

He closes his eyes, and is breathing deeply in two heartbeats. I get the impression Mr. Pettigrew is missing some shuteye these nights.

I make my way to the door as there's a bench just outside on the boardwalk, and plop down thereon with the paper to entertain. Two women, in bustled calico dresses pass, but I pay them little attention, except for an admiring glance, a demure smile, and a tip of the hat. Nemesis has become a bustling place, with ore wagons heading for a mill I noticed some distance from town, farm wagons, a buggy, and a few horsebackers.

I'm just completing an article about the outlaw Jessie James robbing a bank in Columbia, Kentucky, and just into one about the eruption of the volcano, Vesuvius in far off Italy, when I realize the street traffic has disappeared, and the street's gone silent. I look up and am surprised to see five armed men abreast, only a block away, marching with determination down the center of the dusty main street.

They are coming our way, and look to have evil intent.

## CHAPTER FOUR

After the demonstration of his skill and
courage last night, I'm surprised when I
awaken Mr. Pettigrew, inform him of the
approach of the five men, and he hits the
floor running — not to meet them, but out
the back of the barber shop. It appears he's
not pleased to be outnumbered.

Not that any sane man would be.

"I believe I'll excuse myself as well," Andy,
the barber, says, fitting a floppy felt hat in
place, then adds, "I'll leave you the rifle,"
and he, too, disappears into a back room
and I hear an unseen door open and slam.
I'm wondering what the hell I need the rifle
for, as to date, it's not my fight.

Just as I decide to return to my bench and
try to look as innocent as possible, a mere
bystander with my nose in the Leslie's
Weekly, to my surprise Mr. Pettigrew bursts
back into the barber shop, only now he carries a Winchester in one hand and that

wicked sawed-off twelve gauge coach gun in the other. His revolver is holstered. I presume he has a mount tied out back.

"You armed?" he asks as he heads for the window to check what he must surmise are his adversaries.

"Vest pocket gun, but unloaded. I tried to hit a rabbit or two with the worthless thing."

He gives me an irritated look, but then studies me and asks, his tone low and serious. "You with me, Mr. Boone?"

I must admit I sigh deeply and dubiously before answering. I don't believe I've ever been asked a more difficult question. Then I buck up. "You did me a kindness, so yes. I don't mind if I do."

He hands me the Winchester, then goes behind the barber chair and fetches the barber's rifle from the corner, asking at the same time, "You a fair shot?"

"I'm still alive after the hostilities and that did not result from missing that at which I aimed. Some far, some close. More than one time I felt the breath of a man I'd holed with my Spencer . . . which I liberated from the hands of a Union gentleman."

"Then let's see what we can stir up outside."

He exits the front door without hesitation, and I take a deep breath and follow as far as the doorway. The five men are only a hundred feet away by this time, and seeing Mr. Pettigrew, pull up, each with a rifle in hand, each with a revolver on his hip.

Mr. Pettigrew steps up beside a six by six inch post holding the porch roof of the tonsorial parlor up, and raises the rifle, obviously zeroing in on one of the men in the street.

None of them look like miners to me, the one on my side looks to be a Mexican with a wide sombrero and cartridge filled bandoleros crossing his chest. He looks more like a Sonoran *soldado* I note as I take a position in the open door of the barbershop, using as much of it as I can for cover.

"Wilkenson!" Mr. Pettigrew shouts. The man in the middle of the five, with flaring pork chop sideburns of silver, a wide girth, and a flat *ranchero*'s hat almost as wide brimmed, spits a mouthful of tobacco in the street.

Then his voice, more a growl than a shout, echoes down the street. "You shot down my boy like he was a lowly cur, Pettigrew. You're gonna die for that. I hope you've had your shave as it will keep the undertaker from having to complete that task. That is if he gets to you before I feed you to the hogs."

"Your boy was a grown man, Wilkenson,

and he brought it on himself. I ran him out of the Angel for palming a card . . . he was lucky I didn't shoot him down right then and there . . . but I just ran him out. It was his mistake coming back, hoot owl drunk, carrying, cocked and ready for bear."

"Don't matter. I'm gonna plant you this very day."

"Go home and think it over. There are men at every second story window. . . ."

Mr. Pettigrew is lying, and I'm sure of it, but Wilkenson and his men are not so sure, and they all worriedly glance up at the second story of the Stockman's Bank and of the Olympic Hotel across the way.

Mr. Pettigrew does not wait, but snaps the Henry to his eye and fires when they're distracted, and a fancy dressed man on the far end of the line does a backward somersault. Pettigrew gets off two shots before I get a bead on a man, now running away. I fire and he flinches, spins, then wavering, heads for an alleyway.

I see one man is down, one disappeared, and three still heading our way at a run, Wilkenson being one of them; they're firing, and glass is shattering and splinters flying all around me as they come. I take a bead on another of them through the gunsmoke filling the street, the Mexican, just as the door jamb near my head splinters and I fire as I jerk away . . . still the man goes down, and I see him pulling himself away, on hands and knees, dragging a leg. He leaves the sombrero behind. Both the other two spin and hightail it to the far side of the street, then into the substantial stone Stockman's Bank building.

"I put one in MacIntosh's pumper," Pettigrew says, his voice a low growl. "How'd you do?"

"I winged one, or maybe better, and knocked the stilt out from under another."

He gives me an admiring look. "Damned if you ain't handy as a pocket in a shirt. MacIntosh was the cock of their chicken coop, a man with a wide reputation, which is why I took him to task first off. He's a pile of chicken shit now, and two more of their shooters are down and likely out. That'll start their sails to luffin'. You earned your keep, Mister."

"Well, I'm not much in a foot race, but I am a fair hand with a firearm."

"Damned if you ain't! I probably should'a shot Wilkenson as they'd likely leave the country with the paymaster toes up. Oh, well . . . never look back. Speakin' of that, go take a look out back. One of them is still on our side of the street, even if he is draggin' a leg, and I don't want him backshootin' me . . . or you."

I do so, and see no one up and down behind the buildings, nothing but trash thrown from the back of the places of business, a few privies, and the kitchen behind the Angel, now serving as my residence.

On my return, I see that Pettigrew is in conversation with a man who's standing in the middle of Main Street, his arms folded, his derby hat cocked to the side.

Pettigrew yells at the man, "You tell them to get the hell out of town, and I won't come looking for old man Wilkenson for a while." Only then do I realize, as he unfolds his arms, that the man is wearing a brass star.

"You'd go looking for a man when you know he has more'n twenty backing him up?" the man with the badge shouts back.

"You know me. More balls than brains. Do I have to answer that, Pete?" When he gets no reply, Pettigrew shouts, "Seems to me he's got his craw full and turned tail. And us an old fat man and a gimp. . . ." He turns to me, "Sorry."

"Truth is what it is," I say with a shrug. However, I never thought of Mr. Pettigrew as fat, although I have thought of myself as a gimp. He is barrel chested, but fat . . . no.

His hair is more gray than black, so old is only somewhat an exaggeration. His mustache, however, is almost white, which is an indicator of some age.

The man he called Pete looks exasperated, then spins and heads for the bank, pausing to kneel by the fallen man Pettigrew had called MacIntosh. Then, shaking his head, he goes on into the bank. It seems a long while, but is only minutes, until he returns and crosses the street and comes right to the door of the barbershop.

"Who's this?" he asks, eyeballing me.

"Mr. Boone. He's a new employee over at the Angel." Pettigrew turns to me. "This is Territorial Marshal Ivan Petrovich Keller, Pete to his friends. An old friend of mine."

I nod, but Keller has already turned his attention back to Pettigrew.

"Friend, hell," the Marshal says, and spits in the street before continuing. "Wilkenson says he's leaving, but he'll take his three shot men to Doc Peabody's first and —"

"He'd better take MacIntosh to the digger. He went down hard."

"He ain't breathing, for what it's worth."

"It's worth plenty to me, the rotten son of a she bitch. You tell Wilkenson to pick up his dead and wounded, but stay in Main Street and we won't lob any more his way."

"Wilkenson said for you to come on out to the mine when you get the chance. He said you won't be livin' long, for what it's worth, so you might as well come on up and take your medicine. Says as soon as he hears I've ridden on, he'll be back to ventilate your ugly hide."

"You tell him I'll be happy to come on out his way, only I'll be spooning out the castor oil. Tell him to tell his men to stay out of the Angel, in fact to walk light in town, if they don't want to join MacIntosh in hell. I won't take kindly to the sight of any Wilkenson Dead Horse Canyon Mine employees, or his sons for that matter."

"You tell him, you want him told. I got to send a wire to Judge Rankin. He'll want to know why we got people to bury."

"People?"

"Yep, one of you gut shot Perry McWilliams, and I'd bet a dollar to a dime he ain't gonna make it. He's gonna die long and hard. And Appy Sanchez, he took one in the leg and he may lose it . . . and it could go green and he'll be fodder as well."

"Couldn't happen to a finer couple of fellows. You tell the judge it was five of them, coming after me and Mr. Boone here, and other than the numbers, it was a fair fight."

"I'm told you fired first?"

"Did you figure they came to parlay? Five rifles aimed at me . . . what did you think I was gonna do . . . dance a jig."

"Maybe I ought to arrest you both here and now."

"Maybe you ought to give it a try. Being in the right, we won't go easy."

There's a long silence before Keller relents. "They did have you severely outnumbered," Keller says, a little sheepishly.

"Ha," Pettigrew snarls, "I meant by a fair fight they didn't bring nearly enough firepower to scrap with Boone and I." He laughs, then adds, "Tell the judge we was in the right."

"That's for the judge to decide," Keller says with a growl, then the marshal stomps away toward the bank, and Pettigrew turns back to me, and for the first time since I've met the man, he smiles broadly. "Winged him, eh? Sounds like you winged his backbone, going through his fat gut first, and did a good job of bringing the saw bones some business, and probably the digger. Next time you see Señor Aparicio Sanchez, you'll be on even footin', so to speak."

For some reason, that makes me grin. "Both of them was fairly large targets, at only thirty or forty paces. Hard to miss by much. I'd have kilt the skinny Mexican one had it not been for the splinters flying in my face."

"Oh, missin's been done oft times a whole lot closer. Let's wander down to the hotel and I'll stand you to four fingers of good whiskey."

"I promised Miss Alice —"

"Miss Alice will be fine with it."

"I could stand to get the taste of gun-smoke out of my throat, but first see if you can dig this splinter out of my neck. Thought at first I was winged."

He investigates the bloody spot on my neck, then digs a folding knife out of a trouser pocket, and then the half inch splinter out of my neck. He fetches a rag off the barber's back counter and hands it to me, just as Andy the barber sticks his head back in the room from the rear. "That was a six dollar window, Mr. Pettigrew. And it seems there's some carpentry needs doin'. That door jamb will need replacing."

Pettigrew looks irritated, then concedes. "Guess we could have wandered out into the street and spared your woodwork at the expense of our hides. None-the-less, I'll send a man over to board the window up until we can get a replacement. Finish my shave, Andy. If I have the pleasure, I'll soon take the cost of all of it out of Wilkenson's fat ass. In fact, maybe I'll bring you one of those fine stained glass windows he has in that castle of his."

"My pleasure finishing the shave, but I don't want no window I can't see through, pretty colors or not." It takes Andy only a couple of minutes to finish up, as I stand guard at the front door.

Pettigrew rises and stretches after he's mopped up the rest of the shaving soap, then gives me a nod. "Might be better we go out the back way. Besides, my horse is tied out there and I need to check on him. It would be just like those no good low life sons a bitches of Wilkensons to shoot an innocent critter just because it belongs to a body. You got a horse . . . course you don't, you rode in on the rail."

"Haven't owned a horse since the plantation. Had a few good ones die under me in the hostilities, but they belonged to the Confederacy."

"Well, sir, I owe you a horse and a rig, and we'll take care of that after we celebrate the fact we got no holes in our hide."

Again, he smiles. I guess it takes ventilating a few hides to make him grin.

I've decided to dig into this man, to see what makes him tick, even if it does raise the hair on the back of his neck. Sounds a little as if he might have been a sailor at one time.

And now seems the time to do so, while he's still got half a smile in him. The hell of it is, I've missed my own shave and trim.

# CHAPTER FIVE

The Royal Olympic Hotel is run by a Greek gentleman, I discover, as Mr. Pettigrew introduces me to Aaegus Papadopolous, known, he quickly informs me, as Aggie to his friends; and every man, he claims, is a friend until proven otherwise.

Aggie introduces me to a drink from his country, ouzo, which scorches my throat like a hot poker. After three shots of the liquid, as hot as the lava of the famous Santorini volcano of his country, my throat has gone numb . . . as has my reticence about questioning Mr. Pettigrew.

Mr. Papadopolous has left us to our own designs at a small table, near the window — at Mr. Pettigrew's insistence — and for the first time, I find Mr. Pettigrew only a small bit on the talkative side. Loquacious he is not, but his tongue is beginning to loosen.

"So," I say after we talk a while, "we have something in common. You fought for the south, as did I, you fought to preserve states rights, not necessarily the institution of slavery, as did I. I always treated my slaves fairly, and found after the hostilities that paying them fairly was about as cheap as keeping them. As did many others. Of course, those were the ones whose slaves stayed with them during this so-called reconstruction. Fact is, many of my fellows continued to work for the northerner to whom I sold our place, or I should say who stole our place . . . work as sharecroppers, but work with the opportunity to better themselves. I left them with my good wishes. So, what brought you west?"

His "almost" smile is working again; not quite a real smile, even though it seems I've ingratiated myself somewhat. He speaks earnestly. "We all seem to have left some things behind we'd prefer not to remember, Mr. Boone. You, injuries to your person, which you cannot run from, as it must haunt you each time you take a step. Me, injuries to my soul, which I may, one day, be able to escape, should there actually be a gracious God in Heaven. Now, that's enough of that."

"Why's that, Mr. Pettigrew? I'm interested in what got you to Nemesis," I say, my ouzo giving me courage I haven't possessed for

51

some time.

"Because I say so, Mr. Boone. If we are to remain friends, and I hope we do, as you seem to be a man who can be counted on, we must each, none-the-less, maintain some privacy."

"So, you have no interest in sharing your troubles with me?"

His look hardens. "I have no interest in sharing my troubles, nor my past, with any living human being. It is, and shall remain, mine to ponder."

"Ponder, or fret about?"

He's beginning to stroke his mustache, which I've come to learn means considerable irritation.

I eyeball him carefully for a full half-minute, then decide discretion the better part of valor, and change the subject. "Doesn't matter what you share. This above all else, to thine own self be true. Then, let's have another shot of this Hades' piss and then I must get to work."

He almost smiles again. "I should caution you, Mr. Boone . . . Mr. Wilkenson is a no-good lying son-of-a-whore who is most likely laying out in the weeds with a Sharps, waiting to make a mush mess out of your fine southern head. He's a grinder when it comes to grudges, and you don't want to be grist for his mill. So tread lightly."

I toast him with my new shot of ouzo, and he returns the favor with a clink of shot glasses. Now with enough of the hot liquor in my gut, I become a philosopher. "And I should caution you, Mr. Pettigrew, if I may be so bold . . . I'm beyond giving a tinker's damn if he makes mush of mine, or that I pulverize his. And that, sir, puts him at a severe disadvantage. I may not be as fast as the average man, but I'm damn sure more reckless. For as God is my witness, I don't give a hoot nor a holler if I live nor die."

"Then, sir," he says, his eyes taking on a bit of a sad hound-dog look, "we have something more in common. We must be careful or we'll rule the world, for indifference is something to fear mightily. A man with nothing to lose can be a terrible adversary."

He gives me a crooked smile. "You speak with considerable eloquence, Mr. Boone."

I give him a lopsided grin in return, and lather it on even more. "I never did know so full a voice issue from so empty a heart. But the saying is true, the empty vessel makes the greatest sound."

The fourth shot is smooth and soft as a plump woman's breast, and I decide right then and there that this ouzo stuff is seriously dangerous, as is any potion which leads one to tell the whole truth.

The good of it is, it seems Mr. Pettigrew and I understand each other.

When we return to the Angel, Miss Alice is obviously irritated, but Mr. Pettigrew speaks up before she has a chance to chastise me. I am one half hour late.

"I presume that gunfire was you?" she addresses Mr. Pettigrew.

"Now, lass, why would you presume such a thing?"

"Because the smithy ran in here and said it was you, and because ninety five percent of all gunfire happening in Nemesis seems to come from your firearms . . . that's why."

"Humph," Mr. Pettigrew manages, then replies, "Wilkenson and some of his hired help took offence at me shooting his boy full of square nails."

"So, you decided to shoot some more at Wilkenson for good measure?"

"Nope, I took the most dangerous of the bunch out first, MacIntosh, that lousy lowland Scot buggerer of sheep, whose fame seemed larger than his skill, as seems to be the case with most gunfighters' reputations . . . and Mr. Boone here followed suit with a couple more of those fine fellows, one of which for sure is toes up."

I'm embarrassed for Mr. Pettigrew, as his language was such as should never be used in a lady's presence.

"The hell you say," she says, and, in turn, centering yellow eyes on mine. I blush for her. I believe that's the first time I've ever heard a woman swear, or listen to such language as Mr. Pettigrew's without a blush. Then she adds, turning to me, "I thought you was gonna get a shave and trim? You've been gone long enough to have a new suit of clothes sewn."

I start to speak, but Mr. Pettigrew again beats me to it. "Odds are Mr. Boone saved my hide, so let's go a little easy on him. If you allow him an early supper break, I'll buy him a shave and haircut, and something more to boot."

"Humph," she says, hands on hips. "As long as he's back in time to sit shotgun. We should have a house full tonight."

"So, I got the job?" I ask.

"You do, and it's worth a dollar and a half a day, four bits more'n swamping, as you're likely to get your hide ventilated."

"Suits me," I say, and she shakes her head and walks away toward the door leading to the kitchen.

"Miss Alice," Pettigrew stops her short.

"You were paying that last scalawag, Cyrus what's-his-name, two a day. Mr. Boone here did save my bacon."

"Pet," she says sharply, "there are times a body should mind their own business." Then she turns to me again. "Two dollars a day, but you damn sure will earn it."

"Yes, ma'am," I say. I've suddenly become a man of some means. Now all I've got to do is stay alive until payday rolls around, whenever that might be.

# CHAPTER SIX

Now shaved and trimmed, and in possession of a fine blood red gelding and only slightly worn saddle and bridle, thanks to Mr. Pettigrew's generosity, I'm a new man, and gainfully employed, sitting shotgun. I also have new accommodations. It seems a room in the cellar of the Olympic fits my income, as it's shared with at least four other fellows from time to time. Two double beds and a single are spaced out . . . and I'm able to take the single, with my own thunder pot and small chest to store my belongings, not that I have any to store.

I'm happy to say the Chinaman who brought me my steak last night is assigned the swamping chores, as I am perched just beyond the end of the bar against the back wall, with my back literally against the wall, on a waist high backless stool, a double barrel scattergun casually across my knees. No one other than the little Chinaman, who is called Wong, and the two girls working the room, have spoken to me all evening, although many eyed me up and down, seeming to take my measure.

And I eyed them right back with my best glower.

The taller of the two ladies working the room has introduced herself as Martha Ann, and promptly informed me that she didn't mind a man of light weight even if one legged on her belly, so long as he had a token which could be purchased from the bartender for a single dollar, which turned me a rosy shade but did bring me a grin. The other, Blossom, is a half head shorter and of more generous proportions, doe brown eyes that show a soft soul, but with a ready smile and a giggle that can't help but make a body grin ear to ear. She smells of cinnamon, always a favorite of mine.

It is, however, my instruction to keep a serious demeanor and a constant eye out for trouble — as a man with a grin lacks fearsomeness, and it's my job to instill caution in the customers. The night, however, is quiet, with not so much as a voice raised in anger.

It is the easiest money I've ever earned, but I figure that every night might not come along as peacefully.

Early the next morning I find myself seated with Miss Alice and Mr. Pettigrew, enjoying coffee and some of Miss Penellope Jane's hot-out-of-the-grease sugared donuts, when a young man enters the Angel. He's sporting a black derby hat, a starched collar, and a green garter on each sleeve of a white shirt with thin black stripes, and walks straight to our table.

"Morning," he says, snatching the derby off, eyeing the plate of donuts.

"Take a seat, Charley," Miss Alice instructs him, then turns to me.

"Beau Boone, this is Charley Snodgrass, who runs the station and the telegraph, and it's a fine job he does."

We shake, and Charley sits, his eyes hardly leaving the plate. Finally, he turns to Mr. Pettigrew, who's been watching Charley with some amusement, and suggests, "Mr. Pettigrew, I'll trade you some information of interest for one of those donuts, and maybe a beer after work."

Mr. Pettigrew gives him a hard look. "Well, Charley, them are not my donuts. They are the property of Miss Alice here, so I guess I got nothing to trade."

"But I'll stand you to one, Charley," Miss Alice says, with a chuckle.

It's obvious, trade or not, Charley wants

to tell what he knows. Mr. Pettigrew shrugs, "So, what's this information?"

"Wilkenson came to the office before he left town and sent a telegram. I normally don't share folks private business, but this seems a vile affair."

Again, Mr. Pettigrew shrugs.

So Charley continues, "Sent to Denver."

"And that concerns me how?" Mr. Pettigrew asks, seeming to be a little irritated as Charley chews while he talks, his mouth stuffed.

"Arless Blackthorne," Charley says, mumbling a little.

"Arless Blackthorne," Mr. Pettigrew repeats, then turns to Miss Alice. "Is that the Blackthorne I think it is?"

"Must be. Did some time as a lawman down in Texas." Miss Alice is searching her mind, then adds, "got invited out of Houston, got run out of New Orleans, said to have killed more than a dozen men. He has some reputation as a bounty hunter, but more as a hired gun."

"So," Mr. Pettigrew asks, "what was the gist of this communication?"

"Wilkenson is hiring him, presuming he'll take a thousand dollars plus expenses to come to Nemesis and clear out some vermin."

"Well, that's good to know," Mr. Pettigrew says. "I presume Mr. Boone here and myself are to be the subjects of this vermin control venture." Mr. Pettigrew seems amused, while I'm a bit offended. He continues, "Have another donut, Charley, and I will stand you to that beer after you close up. You have my thanks."

Charley nods, stands, grabs another treat, and heads for the door.

Seemingly with an afterthought, Mr. Pettigrew jumps to his feet and follows Charley, and I overhear him ask, "Charley, there's something you can do for me. . . ." Then they disappear out the batwings.

Mr. Pettigrew returns without explanation, and retakes his seat.

Miss Alice takes a deep breath, and looks at Mr. Pettigrew with some sadness; her yellow eyes seem to soften. "Pet, will this never end?" she asks.

"Life goes on, lass. Until it don't no more."

"Well, Pet, that's a real piece of insight." She sighs deeply before continuing. "Why don't you climb on the train and head for San Francisco and see if you can find me a nice boarding house to buy. Something that I can grow old with, without having to dodge buckshot and put up with drunks.

I'm pretty sick of all this."

Mr. Pettigrew gives her an equally sad smile in return; he covers one of her hands with his. "That sounds fine to me, Alli, me love." Then he adds, "soon as I conclude this business with Wilkenson. I don't want to be looking over my shoulder the rest of my life."

"And I don't want to go to San Francisco alone."

He pats her hand. "Darlin', fate smiles on me, you know that."

"If fate's a lady, darlin', then, darlin', she gets tired, just like the rest of us."

"One more time, sweet Alice, one more time."

Alice stands, slipping her hand out from under Mr. Pettigrew's. "I've got to go to Jake's for some groceries."

"I'll come along to carry," Mr. Pettigrew says, and starts to rise.

"I don't need help," Miss Alice snaps, and he slumps back into his seat, seemingly rebuffed. She spins on a heel and heads for the door, speaking back over her shoulder. "You two enjoy those sweets as they may be your last, if this Blackthorne fella stands up to his reputation."

"Don't buy us a pine box quite yet," Mr. Pettigrew yells after her and she pushes through the batwings, then he turns to me. "Hell, we might as well clean them up. No sense in them going to waste." Then he chuckles, and adds, "It ain't like we're gonna die of natural causes."

# CHAPTER SEVEN

Saturday night seemed strangely quiet. I don't know if the populace expected a visit by Caleb Wilkenson and his sons, but they stayed away from the Angel Saloon. In fact, so quiet, I caught myself dozing and almost fell off my stool, which is a mite precarious for a one legged man in any case.

There is no church in Nemesis, or I'd consider going this Sunday morn. It seems the Mexican who I shot in the leg passed in the night, from loss of blood or so the doc reported, so I could likely use some forgiveness. They had one but it burned down, or so I've been told, a bit less than a year ago on July 4th, due to some over exuberant use of fireworks.

I'm also informed that Miss Alice lives in what was once the rectory, the former preacher's residence, a small cottage out back of what is now only a stone foundation some twelve paces wide by twice that long. The rest of the charcoal mess has been long ago cleaned away, and now a vegetable and flower garden resides inside and outside what's now only a low stone wall, with a three foot wide opening where the access under the church floor once was only a darkened hole.

It seems that Mr. Pettigrew comes and goes from the cottage at regular intervals, entering in the evening and leaving at sun up. I have never asked Miss Alice her last name, but presume as she's called "Miss" that it's not Pettigrew. To each his, or her, own.

I have, only this morning, been invited to take a room on the top floor of the Olympic. It's a garret room, which is to my liking, with a wide window with access to the roof, which in turn is a short drop to an outside landing and stairway. I have negotiated the price with Mr. Papadopolous, and am paying only thirty five cents a day, only a dime more than I paid to share a room with three who generally snored like a den of grizzly bears.

The room is not large, a single wide bed with hardly more width than that again, but it has a four drawer dresser, a rack on the wall for hats and such, a single ladder back chair at the foot of the bed, and the garret window has a two foot wide sill that readily hosts a white pitcher and bowl — I'm living the life of a potentate.

However, a potentate probably doesn't have to look forward to his town filling with ranchers and miners from the outlying area, as it's this afternoon that Rosco Wilkenson will be celebrated with a meeting on the only patch of grass in Nemesis, which is next to the railroad station.

It's our understanding that a barrel of decent whiskey and several kegs of beer will be provided for the throng expected to attend.

Mr. Pettigrew has spent most the morning sitting quietly in a corner of the saloon, reading. I can't help but notice that his Winchester and sawed off shotgun are both close at hand, resting in the corner behind his chair, and his revolver is strapped to his waist.

Having high hopes of working my new bay horse out with a ride to the country, I quickly changed my mind when I learned of the funeral celebration.

Mid-morning, Mr. Pettigrew waves me over, and advises, "Judge Isaiah T. Rankin is due in on the eleven o'clock from the east and wants to sit with us a spell. I suggested, via the wire, that we lunch at the Olympic, and you're to be in attendance."

I merely nod, and return to my stool, not that there's any threat to the place as Mr. Pettigrew, Horace the bartender, and Blossom, one of the doves who works the place, are the only warm bodies present. Blossom plays a solitaire game in a corner away from Mr. Pettigrew, Horace is busy shining glasses, and I'm engaged with a new Leslie's Weekly, when we hear heavy foot falls on the boardwalk outside.

I have the Leslie's across the shotgun in my lap, and notice that Mr. Pettigrew reaches back and retrieves the sawed off and places it in his lap under the table, out of sight.

Seeing three large men pass the one of the large windows flanking the batwing doors, I go ahead and cock both barrels of the shotgun.

But two of them remain just outside the doors, while the third pushes his way inside.

Mr. Pettigrews voice rings out, low and cold. "I thought I told you boys to stay the hell out of the Angel."

I recognize the barrel chested man. It's the stud horse himself, Caleb Wilkenson.

He hasn't seen Pettigrew at first, who's perched in the front corner opposite the bar, but turns to the voice.

"I just dropped by to let you know that you're not welcome at this funeral."

Pettigrew makes a sound a bit like a low chuckle, then adds, "Don't worry, I won't be there to pray for Rosco."

"Won't be a lot of praying. Will be a lot of drinking, and some eatin', as there's a pig on the spit down there that's been turning since sunup."

"I smelled the stink," Mr. Pettigrew says.

Wilkenson ignores him and continues. "So don't you, or any of the riffraff from this place, show your face."

"Wouldn't think of it," Pettigrew says.

Wilkenson turns back toward me. "That goes for you, too, Boone," then to Patty, "And that whore," then to Horace, "And, you, you thieving barkeep."

"That's enough, Wilkenson," Mr. Pettigrew snaps. "Get out, stay out. Tell the drunks who've come to see your boy off to hell that they aren't welcome here this day."

"Humph," Wilkenson says, and spins on his heel and pushes out.

The wake, funeral, drunken assembly, is well under way when Mr. Pettigrew and I walk over to the Olympic to join Judge Isaiah T. Rankin for lunch. His honor is not present when we enter, not by the time we finish two mugs of beer, nor when we finally order our lunch. There is no competition for service, as we are the only patrons in the establishment.

Mr. Papadopolous informs us he has purchased a fresh mule deer carcass from a passing hunter and we are served an excellent venison stew and some hard crusted bread to go along with our third mug of suds, and we are scraping the bottom of our bowls when the judge makes his appearance.

A man of generous girth, and better dressed even than Mr. Pettigrew, with a cutaway coat and waistcoat to match, he has to push his chair well back to be seated, after he and I had said our greetings. He eyes me carefully after he's been seated, and not with admiration, then he turns to Mr. Pettigrew.

"You've shot a few more fellas dead, haven't you, sir."

"No deader than they deserved, Judge," Mr. Pettigrew answers, giving the judge as hard a stare in return as he'd gotten.

"As I understand it, Wilkenson's son . . . this Rosco fella, came at you with a weapon, but the others were merely strolling down the road."

Pettigrew was silent for a moment. "I

presume you stopped by the gathering and took advantage of the pig before you kept your appointment?"

"I did, but I can dine again, if you're in the buying mood."

"The venison stew is more than respectable, and I'll be happy to match Wilkenson's donations dollar for dollar."

The judge's look hardens. "Are you insinuating that I can be bought, Pettigrew?"

"I merely stated a fact, judge. Dollar for dollar."

The judge turns and yells to Mr. Papadopolous, who is seated across the room, reading a newspaper. "Aggie, I don't suppose you've got a chunk of the loin off that deer?"

"I do, judge," he calls back.

"A fat chunk, medium rare, blackened, with some fried potatoes, and a good chunk of that hard bread I see the remnants of all over this table."

"Yes, sir . . . er . . . judge, it's the same price as beef tenderloin."

"Price is no object, Aggie. My associate here, Mr. Pettigrew, has offered to stand me to lunch." Then he again studies each of us carefully, then as an afterthought, turns back to the proprietor as he is leaving for the kitchen. "Aggie, bring me three fingers

70

of that good brandy, if you would be so kind."

"My pleasure."

Again he turns and eyes each of us, then announces, "Marshal Keller is insisting that I indict you and Mr. Boone here for murder."

"And you say?" Pettigrew asks, very quietly.

"I say I want to chat with all concerned before I take such drastic action."

I decided I've been quiet long enough. "They were coming at us with gun in hand, judge. Are you a fan of the bard?"

"The bard?"

"Master Shakespeare. If you prick us, do we not bleed? If you tickle us, do we not laugh? If you poison us, do we not die? And if you wrong us, shall we not revenge? I'd say coming at us, crying threats, guns in hand, constitutes a wrong in any man's book."

"All that's neither here nor there. They were carrying rifles . . . did you expect them to be stuffed down a pant leg, Mr. Boone?"

"I have an excellent memory, judge, and not only for the works of the bard. Before any gunfire was exchanged, Mr. Wilkenson said, and I quote, 'I'm gonna feed you to the hogs . . . you're gonna die . . . I'm gonna plant you this very day' . . . and some other threat before any gunfire was exchanged. I would say Mr. Pettigrew was very patient, considering five heavily armed men were bearing down upon the two of us."

"And who fired first?" the judge asked, glaring at me.

# Chapter Eight

"When there are five guns trained on you and gunfire erupts, it's unlikely one would remember the difference of a split second. It was Bull Run or Antetium out there in the street for a few moments, judge. You'd probably get a dozen different stories should you interview a dozen different men . . . and all would be different."

"That doesn't answer the question, Mr. Boone. Who fired first?"

I clear my throat before answering, and consider my words carefully, then say as quietly as Mr. Pettigrew had, "there's no question who fired the straightest, even if not first."

"Humph," he says, then the conversation is interrupted by Mr. Papadopolous appearing with a generous glass of brandy.

Mr. Pettigrew rises and extends a hand to the judge. "Your honor, I've got to get back to the Angel. I'll be dealing faro this evening.

Why don't you drop in and play a few hands. You're looking particularly lucky this afternoon."

That brings a smile to the judge's face for the first time since he's entered the room. He rises, and shakes, then nods and says, "Why, I don't mind if I do. I look lucky, do I?"

"Damned lucky. See you tonight."

And with that, we leave, Mr. Pettigrew paying Papadopolous on the way out, and telling him that he'll pick up the judge's tab for the rest of the afternoon.

We have a crowd with all spots at the wheel taken and both faro tables surrounded with players when the judge ambles in; three dealers have all they can handle. I recline on my stool at the end of the bar, scatter-gun across my thighs, and Mr. Pettigrew sits in his front corner, his back to the wall as usual, his sawed off coach gun near at hand.

The judge runs a finger in the pocket of his embroidered waistcoat and fishes out a coin as he approaches the bar. I take it upon myself to give Horace a holler, and he comes far enough my way that I can give him a quick heads up that he is not to charge the judge.

Ordering a shot of the best whiskey in the house, his honor gives me a nod when Horace won't take his money. Mr. Pettigrew has spotted him as well, and rises to join him at the bar for some low conversation.

It is only a short time when they both rise and cross the room to the nearest faro table. I can see plenty of displeasure among the players when Mr. Pettigrew shuts the table down, takes the dealer's position, and allows the judge to be the sole player in the game.

Porter Moscovitch, the displaced dealer, walks through the crowd and joins me at the closest seat. I've traded few words with the faro dealers as both are only part time employed, working Friday and Saturday nights — Miss Alice often deals when midweek — while Porter and Aleandro, the other dealer, are otherwise employed in town as day bartenders in other establishments — one at the Olympic Hotel and one two blocks away at Bohanna's Pleasure Parlor, commonly known as Bo's Brothel to those who might have that predilection.

"The good judge must be in need," Porter says to me in a low voice.

"Oh, is this a common thing?" I ask.

"Almost every time he's in Nemesis," he says. "Costs me money."

"How's that?"

"I get no tips while Pettigrew is sloppin' the hogs."

I laugh at that, but he doesn't.

I watch carefully for a half hour as Pettigrew deals, and the judge rakes in his winnings. Mr. Pettigrew is a fine master of the cards, as I never see what I would consider a manipulation of the cardboards, yet it must have been happening. Seldom in a lifetime would one win that many hands.

Particularly as the honorable judge consumes at least a dozen three-finger shots of good whisky while doing so. The average man would have been on the floor, but the judge is of generous girth and seems to have a great capacity, not only for unfairly winning, but for the sauce.

I do notice Miss Alice, who keeps moving among the customers giving them smiles and nods; but when she glances at the table where Mr. Pettigrew is feeding dollars to the good judge, her yellow eyes flash fire and she looks a little more than merely irritated, but quickly mellows when her attention is turned to other customers.

It is my estimate that Judge Isaiah Rankin has pocketed at least two hundred dollars when Mr. Pettigrew indicates that the game is over and they both rise and take Porter's seat and one next to it, while Porter returns to his position behind the faro table. The judge seems a bit out of sorts, and Mr. Pettigrew a bit irritated when they take positions at the bar near enough that I can hear their every word.

The judge eyes me, but says nothing, so I cut my eyes to the room, which I am being paid to watch no matter what else is underway.

"Why'd you cut me off?" the judge asks Mr. Pettigrew, his words only slightly slurred.

"You pocketed at least two and a quarter, Isaiah. I'd think that enough for one night's play. You're one lucky fellow."

The judge glares at him, then says in a low tone, "I'll be heading up to the mine tomorrow to interview some of Wilkenson's men. You know, Pettigrew, there could still be an inquest. Odds are there will be."

To Mr. Pettigrew's credit, he merely smiles at the judge, and offers his glass in toast. "Here's to your good judgment, judge, and my belief that you will do the right thing."

"Humph," the judge manages, but does clank glasses. He mumbles, "I agree with at least half that statement. We'll see what Caleb has to say on the matter."

"Caleb is it? When did you get so friendly with Wilkenson?"

"He's a generous sort, Pettigrew. You should take note of his generosity."

Mr. Pettigrew answers that with a smile as tight as a cobra's, then waves Horace over. "Give his honor here anything he wants." Then Pettigrew nods to the judge, and returns to his ladderback chair in the front corner opposite the bar.

Pettigrew only remains there for a short while. I sense he is angry, as his jaw remains knotted. Finally, he arises, passes near enough to Miss Alice that he stoops to whisper in her ear, receives a somewhat curt nod in return, then makes his way out the back door. I presume he is headed for their shared cottage behind the ruins of the church.

With the exception of one small scuffle between a drover and a muleskinner, without the involvement of weapons so not requiring my intervention, the night remains uneventful.

The judge stumbles out after having at least a half dozen more drinks.

Mr. Pettigrew, Miss Alice, and myself are enjoying a fine slice of coffee cake, the morning sun not yet over the yardarm, when Andy McBride, the barber, pushes through the batwings, his face white and him talking so fast the spittle is flying from the gap in his missing tooth and us only able to catch about every third word.

"Slow down, Andy," Miss Alice chastises, "And sit down here for a cup of coffee and piece of breakfast cake."

He does so.

"Now," Miss Alice asks, "what's this about the judge?"

"Dead . . . dead as Abe Lincoln, and shot just like him, plus had his throat slit."

# CHAPTER NINE

Miss Alice's jaw drops, as does mine. Mr. Pettigrew, I can't help but notice, seems less than surprised and never brakes his chewing.

"What in the world . . . ?" Miss Alice manages.

"Exactly what happened?" I ask.

"He was found on the other side of the Olympic this morning. Marshal Keller is there now. Someone shot the judge dead center in the back of his head, and cut his throat from ear to ear. Marshal thinks he was shot first as he didn't bleed much for a sliced throat."

"Robbery, I imagine," Mr. Pettigrew manages between bites.

"Don't know," Andy says. "I hear tell he was drunk as a lord when he left here last night."

Mr. Pettigrew smiles, then swallows before adding, "I wouldn't know. I left well before he did and headed home for some shuteye."

I notice Miss Alice cut her eyes at Mr. Pettigrew, but she says nothing to him, then turns to Andy. "Well, it's a damn shame. I do know he left here with a pocket full of money. He won big at faro and, as usual, didn't buy a soul a drink nor pay a dime for his."

"As usual," Mr. Pettigrew manages between bites.

He follows his bite with a sip of hot coffee, when the batwings swung aside again, and Territorial Marshal Keller strides in.

"You heard?" he asks, eyeing the three of us as Andy gives up his seat, tips his hat, and leaves.

"Andy just gave us the news," Miss Alice says. "Sit down, marshal, you look like you could use a cup of coffee."

"No, thanks, I've got to go to the telegraph and get the news out."

"Damn shame," Mr. Pettigrew says, shaking his head, but he appears less than sincere to me.

"You don't own a small caliber weapon, do you, Pettigrew?" the marshal asks, his voice as hard as flint.

"Mr. Colt's .44 revolver and the scattergun," he replies, with a smile.

"And you, Boone?"

81

"I have a pocket pistol, but haven't fired it in a month of Sundays. In fact, haven't had the cartridges to do so since I've come to town. Fired my last cartridge at a rabbit over two months ago. I had nothing against the judge."

Mr. Pettigrew smiles then says, "Damn near everyone in the territory had something against the judge. Boone here was probably the only one for a hundred miles who had no reason to shoot the bastard."

I give him a tight smile. " 'Cept he was thinking of indicting me along with Mr. Pettigrew here. . . ." It probably wasn't a smart thing to say, but it was the truth.

The marshal turns his attention to Miss Alice. "I don't imagine you were too happy about the judge taking a pile of money off your faro table."

She shrugs. "A common occurrence here, marshal, as you know. We run an honest house, and often someone takes a pile of money off our tables."

Keller's gaze shifts from one of us to the other, then, with an audible "humph," he spins on his heel and stomps out.

When he is gone, Miss Alice rises and glares at Mr. Pettigrew. "I hope you at least got the money back . . ." she snaps.

Then she heads for the back door, leaving

Mr. Pettigrew still casually chewing his cake and sipping his hot coffee.

I sit a moment and chew my last bite of cake, then raise my eyes to Mr. Pettigrew. "You didn't really kill the som'bitch, did you?"

"If'n I did, I don't think I'd be mouthin' it about." He smiles again, then adds, "I imagine it was some no good scum-suckin' thief." He shrugs then adds, "Everyone in the saloon saw Rankin shove that two hundred in his pocket, and everyone knew he was drunk as a goat. Two dozen or more saw it. Only makes sense . . . some robber."

I eye him carefully, wondering where the truth is, then offer, "Makes sense to me."

He changes the subject. "So, you seem to be limping less. Is the leg getting tougher?"

"It is. This job of plopping my butt on a barstool seems to favor its healing. I should tell you again, I appreciate what you and Miss Alice have done for me."

He chuckles, then turns serious. "You'll damn sure have a way to earn your money. It's every two weeks or so that some blood is spilled in this house of angels . . . although I doubt if many of those dispatched here, and there have been a half dozen or so in the last two years, have gone in the angel direction. Don't get too comfortable on that stool as, odds are, gunsmoke will fill the air a'fore long."

As I'm about to excuse myself, Charley Snodgrass from the railroad station pushes through the doors, hat in hand.

"He's here," Charley sputters, as if he's announcing the second coming.

Mr. Pettigrew glances up, and gives Charley a smile. "You interested in a piece of this fine cake, Charley?"

"Sure . . . but you should know, he's here."

"He who?" Mr. Pettigrew asks, but it's obvious to me he knows exactly of whom Charley speaks.

"Why, that gunman from Salt Lake City. Blackthorne. Carrying a new Henry rifle, a fancy belt with two holsters slung over his shoulder. Swinging a carpet bag that could hold a dozen more weapons. A couple of boys from Dead Horse Canyon Mine . . . Wilkenson's boys, I think . . . picked him up a half hour ago. I'd a come sooner but I had passengers to attend."

Mr. Pettigrew again smiles. "Impressive, was he. Giant of a fella I imagine."

"Actually he was kinda average looking, except for that engraved belt and holster."

"And how would I recognize Mr. Blackthorne, should he come callin'?"

"Black hair, but with a streak of gray down

84

the middle."

"Kinda like a skunk?" Mr. Pettigrew says, obviously amused by his own humor.

"I don't think I'd be describing him that'a'way, at least not to his face."

Mr. Pettigrew laughs at that, then rises. "You want that cake or not, Charley. It's on the house."

Charley nods, and pulls a red and white checkered neckerchief from his back pocket and hands it to Mr. Pettigrew. "Can you wrap it in that. I gotta get back to the station." But Pettigrew ignores it, looking at the rag like it was something Charley used to wipe his nose, which it probably was.

"I'll have someone bring it out. Thanks for stopping by, Charley." Pettigrew heads out the back.

Shoving my way to stand, I speak for the first time. "Did Blackthorne leave town with the boys from the Dead Horse?"

"They headed for the bank."

"I'd have Horace bring you a cup of coffee, but you're headin' back?"

"I am."

"Thanks for comin' over, Charley."

As it might pay for me to recognize Arless Blackthorne, and as I've become a man of some means, I decide it's time for me to open a savings account at the local banking

establishment. I yell at Horace, the bartender, informing him that I'll be gone for a
half hour, and head for Stockman's, a shiny
dollar in my pocket to begin saving my
fortune.

# Chapter Ten

I've been trying to navigate the world without my cane, as my stub is becoming less and less tender, but take it in hand to cross the oft times rutted road to where the solid stone building — its upper floor being wood frame and board and batt— that was the Stockman's Bank sits across from the Olympic Hotel.

As it happens, I brushed shoulders with a gentleman with a silver steak in his hair as I enter the bank and he is leaving with a pair of young men with the same barrel body shape as Caleb Wilkenson. I presume these are sons of his, as I know him to have four other than the one Mr. Pettigrew shot down in the street.

I tip my hat, and get nothing but disdain in return. Mr. Wilkenson is obviously as remiss in teaching his sons manners as he is in teaching them skill with a firearm.

It's hard not to notice the wad of paper

money the man I presume to be Arless Blackthorne has clutched in one hand. Blackthorne appears no more than average size, but he has quick eyes and a set to his jaw that makes him seem more formidable than the average man.

Moving on to the counter, I am greeted by a young man in a green visor with a purple garter on both sleeves of a starched white shirt with maroon stripes, whom I presume to be the teller, and note another gentleman, even better dressed, at a desk behind. I had been informed that a Simon Chastaine was the bank manager, and that Mr. Chastaine was an employee of the bank's owner, one Caleb Wilkenson.

The teller greets me politely, and I advise, "My business would be with the manager, young man." I have not seen the teller around, and consequently presume him a teetotaler. He turns and speaks to the man I presume to be Chastaine. I did see him in the Angel on my first night there — the night Rosco Wilkenson was killed — but he is not a regular and I don't know him by name. Of course after the conflict in the street outside those associated with Wilkenson have been as sparse in the Angel as politicians' honesty.

Chastaine looks up, then in a voice loud

enough for all to hear, announces, "Mr. Boone's business is not welcome here, Hector. Escort him out."

I shouldn't be surprised, but I am, and momentarily flustered. I had removed my hat, so I reposition it, then a little fire floods my backbone as a result of the insult and I can feel the heat in my ears, and I announce right back, "If that be the case, I don't suppose you'd like your plow cleaned by a one legged man. I'd be proud to beat you into the mud with this hickory cane. Step outside, Mr. Chastaine, and I'll show you how it's done."

Chastaine is a half head taller than myself, but he wastes no time in rising, positioning his own derby hat square on his head, and without giving me so much as a glance, mumbles to his teller, "Don't let him through the gate, Hector," and heads for the back of the building and I presume out the back door, as I hear a slam that causes the front windows to rattle.

So I tip my hat to a wide-eyed "Hector," and make my way out the front.

As I had excused myself for a full half hour, and my time in the bank was cut short, I make my way to Trader Jake's General Store, which is one of the town's larger buildings, although it is only one story. It lies on the far side of Andy Mc-Bride's Tonsorial Parlor and is a well and evenly white-washed board and bat building with only one pair of show windows flanking the front door.

I have not met the widow woman who runs the place, and thought now, as I am in need of some toiletry items, as good a time as any.

As I enter, an attractive woman about my age walks from a rear room, wiping her hands with a towel. She walks straight to me, and gives me a pleasant smile that crinkles the edges of beautiful deep, penetrating, blue eyes. One thinks of a widow woman as gray and pudgy . . . this one is anything but, although that may be the beginning of gray in her auburn hair.

"You're Mr. Boone, the new shotgun guard at the Angel."

"Yes, ma'am. I am guilty of that."

She extends her hand, much as a man would, and I take it and give her a slight shake. I presume as she has taken on the job of a man, she's also taken on the mannerisms, much as has Miss Alice at the Angel. It is a sign of changing times.

"I wondered when you were going to step in and say hello."

"Well, ma'am, here I am, and hello. I'm

Beau Boone."

"And I'm Jessie Traintor. Formerly Mrs. Jake Traintor, but now the widow Traintor."

As I drop her hand, a youth, his size, I imagine, large for his age as his cheeks still have the pudgy bulge of youth, walks from the back room and calls out, "Ma, I'm going on now. Some of the fellas are going to the river to fish."

"Have you finished cutting that meat?"

"No, you do it."

"No, Alex, you do it as I told you to." She turns to me. "Sorry, . . . these young people now days."

"I'm going to the river," the boy says, his tone more than just a little rude.

"No, you're not."

"See you later, mom," he says.

"Hold it," I command. I clomp my way across the floor, peg and cane, and stop directly in front of where he stands, shoulders thrown back, in the doorway. "Young man, I have not had the pleasure . . . or maybe the displeasure . . . of meeting you. I presume you are this lady's whelp."

"I'm her son," he says, his eyes defiant.

"Then I'd suggest you show her a little respect."

"What business is it of your'n?"

I raise the cane to the level of his belt, and

shake it a little as I speak. "It's what business is it of yours, sir." I put some real emphasis on the "sir."

"I called my pa, 'sir.' And you ain't my pa."

"And that, young man, is God's blessing on me."

He cuts his eyes to his mother. "I'm going."

So I drive stubby end the cane deep into his solar plexus, enough that it folds him.

"Please!" his mother shouts, and hurries to his side as he sinks to his knees.

"I'm sorry, Mrs. Traintor, but I can't abide a rude child. His pride is more hurt than his belly. If you need someone to lay the cane to this one upon occasion, I'll be happy to oblige."

"He's my problem," she snaps, uncertainly, as the boy continues to gasp for breath.

"I didn't hurt the whelp."

"The hell . . ." the boy manages, still gasping.

"Watch your language," she says, turning her attention back to the youth. She helps him his feet, and gives him a slight shove. "Now, go back and finish cutting that meat."

He shrugs, and starts to turn.

"Son," I snap, and he faces me, a little

uncertainly himself this time, so I continue. "It's 'yes, ma'am,' young man."

He eyes me as if it's me he'd like to be cutting, but I again shake the cane at him, ever so slightly. Then he gives me an almost imperceptible nod, and mutters, "Yes, ma'am."

She watches him depart and shakes her head. For a moment I'd thought she was going to be very angry with me, but her look has softened with the boy's "yes ma'am."

"How sharper than a serpent's tooth is it to have a thankless child," I quote from King Lear.

"It is," she says.

"Yes, it is," I say.

"No," she says with a small grin, "the quote is 'it is to have a thankless child.' You said 'is it' not 'it is.' "

I can't help but laugh. "By all that's holy, you are right. It's seldom I have my Shakespeare corrected."

"It's seldom I hear any attempted, so it's so very seldom I have the chance to correct." Her smile is flashing, then she turns serious. "I thank you for your help with Alex. Since his father passed, he's been a bit hard to handle."

Again I smile. "It was my pleasure, Mrs. Traintor. How did you acquire an interest in the bard?"

"I was a teacher when I met Mr. Traintor, and English Literature was a specialty of mine. A better question is how did a shotgun guard come to quote the playwright?"

"My father was a fan, and I heard him quoted daily when I was nothing but a whelp myself. I was fortunate to have a father to take the cane to me when needed . . . and to be truthful, that was oft times. I was a mite high spirited, as seems your son."

"I've had some thoughts of you, Mr. Boone," she says, a twinkle in her eye.

That is somewhat a surprise to me, and I guess I show it in my eyes. "Thoughts, ma'am?"

"Yes, when I heard you were injured in the war. I have something that might be of interest to you."

Aw, I fear it's commerce that encourages her "thoughts," not my manliness. Consarn the luck.

She moves behind a counter and slides open a door and removes a handsome cane with a carved ivory handle in the shape of a duck's neck and head, but one that's rather straight not canted as is the inexpensive bentwood one I carry.

"Is this not a beauty?" she asks.

94

"It is, madam, but there are things I don't have that I need."

"Aw, Mr. Boone, but you don't have this."

I shrug, indicating my disinterest. Then she surprises me by pulling the handle to her and the body of the cane away, exposing a beautiful blade. She fully removes it and there's a well-polished two-foot blade that fits nicely in a sheath, both of which pass as a solid cane. And she's right, it's something I don't have, and suddenly covet.

"And the price?" I ask.

"Don't ask until you see its most interesting feature."

She points to a small opening at the base of the handle, then opens a flap which proves to be the action of a tiny firearm, twenty-two or twenty-five caliber I would guess, and folds a small metal trigger down which snaps into place.

"And it comes with a bullet cast of the proper size. I took it in trade for some farm implements. As I recall I allowed ten dollars for it, but I'll tell you what: I'll give it to you for five as there was considerable profit in the implements . . . and if you don't have the five at hand, I'll extend you credit . . . say a dollar now and a dollar a week."

I can't get my hand in my pocket fast enough to fish out the single dollar I have residing there . . . the dollar I was going to use to open a savings account.

"On one condition," I give her a challenge.

"And that is?"

"That we have lunch on the morrow at the Olympic . . ." She seems taken aback, so I quickly add, "and continue our discussion of the bard. You're welcome to bring the boy along —"

"No," she laughs. "I'd think he'd be poor company, under the circumstances . . . and I'd need someone to watch the shop." Her smile almost melts me. "I'd love to have lunch with you, Mr. Boone. To be truthful, I haven't had the company of a gentleman other than here in the store for these two long years since Mr. Traintor passed. If it suits you, I'd like to make it at one o'clock, as the store occasionally gets busy during the lunch period."

I leave the store the proud owner of an interesting implement, a dollar poorer, and hopefully, a lady friend richer. I am now pleased that Mr. Simon Chastaine saw fit to throw me out of his premises, for had he not, it might have been days before I met the widow Traintor.

# CHAPTER ELEVEN

I knew it was too good to last.

Things were peaceful in the Angel, until a half hour to midnight. The girls had made a half dozen trips each out to the cribs, the tables were full of players, Miss Alice was in a good mood, and Mr. Pettigrew had been sitting quietly in his corner, keeping an eye on things, and slowly sipping good whiskey. I had noticed that although he normally kept it to about three fingers an hour, he seems a little more exuberant this night, and as I've made my normal round each hour — showing off my fancy new cane, without divulging its secrets — and speaking to him with each passing, I find him more and more to be slurring his words.

I presume that is what Arless Blackthorne counts upon, as he enters the bar, appointed with not merely one but two fancy nickel plated Colt Sheriff's models. The little .36 caliber revolvers are light in the hand and quick to handle, but pack enough punch to put a man in the ground with a single shot, should it be well placed. He is stylishly dressed, in black trousers with a light gray stripe, a shirt bleached so white it hurts the eyes, and a black leather vest fully appointed with gold watch and chain — the fob being out of sight in a pocket. His wide brimmed hat resides squarely upon his head, the hatband studded with silver conchos. Boots are shined to a gleam and I presume he's dusted them just before entering.

He is dressed like a man who expects to die on short notice, or to be the center of attention if he lives to receive same.

He pauses, six feet into the room, and scans it carefully until he eyes Mr. Pettigrew in his corner, then seemingly satisfied, proceeds to the bar and in a mannerly way, orders himself a beer.

Mr. Pettigrew, I discovered early on, is not a man to be intimidated, and as soon as the hired shooter has his beer in front of him, rises. He elbows his way across the room and takes up a position to the left of Blackthorne, keeping him between his stool and mine. Blackthorne does not turn at Mr. Pettigrew's approach, but he is studying the mirror behind the back bar; I'm sure he is carefully watching. There are a half-dozen patrons separating Blackthorne and my position. The shooter now has his back to me as he's turned to face his adversary. To my surprise, Mr. Pettigrew left his sawed off resting in the corner, and came armed with only his revolver, and it holstered.

I can not hear what transpires between them, but obviously the patrons nearer can, and all quickly rise from stools or from bar-leaning and move away, some who'd heard the exchange dragging others who had not heard, leaving Mr. Pettigrew and Black-thorne now on their feet, facing each other with only a stride separating them. Black-thorne must surely think he is much faster than Mr. Pettigrew, for neither can possibly miss a shot at such a distance, and a more prudent man would have allowed the chance of an errant shot. He is very sure of himself.

Without hesitation I drop from my stool, leaving my scattergun as Mr. Pettigrew would be caught up in its use, and using my newly acquired cane, move as quickly as possible without making noise, until only a stride separates myself and Blackthorne's back. The room goes quiet about the same time as I arrive in position, and slide my nickel-plated blade from its cane scabbard. I place the tip, rather decisively, at the base of Blackthorne's skull, and he flinches ever so slightly; glancing over at the mirror he sees his predicament. To his credit, he doesn't pale to the white of a lizard's belly as would I under the same predicament.

Leaning forward, I say low enough that other patrons can not hear, "Mr. Blackthorne, it's my job to keep the peace here in the Angel, and I fear you have a mind to disturb it."

"Not if this ugly son of a bitch will step outside," he says, loud enough for the whole room to hear.

"You may be fast with those pistols, Mr. Blackthorne, but not as fast as Mr. Pettigrew and myself with our scatterguns, nor me putting this blade through your neck bone." Then I turn my attention to Mr. Pettigrew. "Would you be so kind as to relieve Mr. Blackthorne of his pistols so I don't have to shove this blade through his spine."

Mr. Pettigrew gets a bit of an evil smile — the tight lips of that same lizard — to go along with the narrowing of his eyes. And he reaches . . . but his evil look is making me uncomfortable as a fair fight is one thing, but I want no part of a murder. And I already suspect Mr. Blackthorne of that capability, and am concerned about my culpability.

He reaches across with both hands and

takes a pistol in each, sliding them out of the holsters, spinning them so the muzzles are now buried in the professional shooter's gut.

Strangely, Blackthorne doesn't sound particularly perturbed. "You know I'll gut shoot you both for this," he says, his snarl low and convincing.

Mr. Pettigrew waves Horace Goodfellow, the bartender, over and hands him the pistols. "Would you hold these for Mr. Blackthorne here, please, Horace. I'll trade you for that beer bung banger you keep back there.

Horace hands Mr. Pettigrew the heavy club. I can see Blackthorne's cheeks knot, as he must suspect he is about to be struck. I shove the blade a fraction of an inch deeper, and he holds both hands out to his side, in supplication.

Mr. Pettigrew smiles more widely and again turns to the bartender. "Top Mr. Blackthorne's beer off, Horace. I don't want him to think us inhospitable."

Horace does so and says, "On the house, Mr. Blackthorne."

The hired shooter seems unimpressed, but reaches his right hand for the glass, cutting his eyes at the drink as he does so. To the surprise of all, Mr. Pettigrew swings the hardwood bat as fast as a desert rattler would strike, cracking it down on the outstretched hand. You can hear bones break, and I wince in sympathy.

Mr. Blackthorne cries out, but a low moan, and covers his crushed right hand with his left and brings it to his chest, an agonized look on his face, and as quickly, Mr. Pettigrew steps back and swings hard, and smashes the left where it lays across the black vest. This time Blackthorne cries out like a hawk screaming for its mate.

He pales, then goes the yellow-green of early aspen leaves, and I fear he is about to lose his consumed beer all over the bar, but he stumbles for the batwing doors, his step wavering, without requesting his firearms back . . . not that he could have held them had he done so.

Clasping both hands to chest he disappears out the batwings.

Mr. Pettigrew gives me a wide grin. "Damned if I don't believe that's the last we'll see of Arless Blackthorne, formerly a shooter of some repute, now a man who can't hold a whisky shot glass."

I'm hoping he's right, but wondering if he's just the first of many shooters as Caleb Wilkenson has very deep pockets.

The rest of the evening proves uneventful,

even though Mr. Pettigrew, unusually jovial, continues to indulge in whiskey. Miss Alice seems perturbed by the whole affair, and more so by Mr. Pettigrew's continued drinking.

She leaves the establishment, alone, shortly after the Seth Thomas on the wall strikes a single bell, signaling one a.m.

For the first time since I'd been in the employ of the Angel, I observe Mr. Pettigrew pay attention to one of the bar girls, Martha Ann, the taller and thinner of the two. To my great surprise, as the Seth Thomas strikes two bells, Mr. Pettigrew, his step wavering considerable, escorts Miss Martha Ann out the back door of the Angel.

As little frightens me at this later stage in life, I show no tremor, but do feel a slight shiver of dread down my backbone. The last thing I want is to be sandwiched between Mr. Pettigrew and Miss Alice, he giving me a hard look, her looking for the truth.

It seems an uncomfortable position for an employee, and that is all I am.

We shut the place down as the Seth strikes three bells, having to usher an equal number of drunks out onto the boardwalk.

I am not looking forward to coffee and sweet breads with my employer and her man friend on the morrow.

*Comme si comme ca,* the French would say. *Que sara sara* the Spanish. But Mr. Shakespeare seemed to always say it so much better than others: when sorrows come, they come not single spies, but in battalions.

It could be a dark day tomorrow . . . although I am looking forward to my lunch with Mrs. Traintor.

# CHAPTER TWELVE

Miss Alice and I are well into our second cup of coffee and an exquisite cinnamon coffee cake, served by Miss Penellope Jane with her normal broad smile, when Mr. Pettigrew enters through the rear door of the saloon. His eyes look like two piss holes in the snow, and his movements are lethargic at best.

He seats himself across from Miss Alice, and yells at Horace, the bartender, for coffee, then winces as if the yell shot pain through his cranium.

If I'm not mistaken, he has on the same clothes as he wore last night.

Miss Alice eyes him so coldly I almost shiver. "You slept elsewhere last night."

"Maybe I should excuse myself," I say and start to rise.

"Stay," Miss Alice commands, and I settle back.

"Slept out in the kitchen. Didn't want

Blackthorne to dry gulch me on the way home."

I can't help but notice that he speaks without looking Miss Alice in the eye.

"Funny, you weren't there when I came by this morning," she says, her words forming icicles as they cross the table. "And it looked to me like Blackthorne couldn't have whipped a two year old when he left here, much less lifted a firearm."

"Headed over to the Olympic for some fresh tomato juice when I woke. Had a bit of a head this morning."

"Right," she said, but it was obvious she was onto him. I have no idea where this is going, but know I want no part of it. There's no way for me to win in this situation.

So I rise. "I gotta go over to the bank —"

"Thought they threw you outta the bank," Miss Alice snaps, before I get halfway to my feet.

"The general store, I mean . . . the general store."

She eyes me carefully before she speaks. "You close up last night?"

"Yes, ma'am. You told me I had to stay till the last dog died."

"I want to talk with you later."

"Yes, ma'am." I skedaddle away, but not before I hear her call to Horace.

"Horace, tell the girls to come find me soon as they show up this afternoon."

"Yes'um," he answers.

Mr. Pettigrew sits quietly through this exchange, then rises and walks to the bar, where Horace is pouring his mug of coffee.

It seems Miss Alice will not be one to be cuckolded. I'm glad all I can testify to is Mr. Pettigrew and Martha Ann heading out the door together . . . and I'll quit this fine paying job before I flap my lip to Miss Alice in that regard. However, it may be that the two of them, Mr. Pettigrew and Martha Ann, may just be in the eye of the hurricane.

For the rest of the morning, Miss Alice parks herself in the corner working on her books; Mr. Pettigrew disappears out the back door, I presume to catch up on his sleep; and I help Horace clean up the bar and polish the mirrors. That is, until Miss Alice folds up her journals and calls me over to her corner. Somehow I feel as if I'm climbing the hangman's scaffold, and I'm the one with his hands bound behind his back.

I sit across from her and wait with some trepidation.

"You've proven yourself to be a truthful man, Beau, and I'm going to ask you straight out . . . do you know where Pet slept last night?"

It was a question I can answer truthfully. "I have no idea, ma'am. I presumed he was headed for your cottage."

"He wasn't . . . nor did he arrive there. So, where?"

If I had a Bible I could swear upon it. "As God is my witness, I have no idea where he might have slept."

Again she gives me a hard look. "Do you have a suspicion?"

"Ma'am, I learned many a year ago to only act on fact."

"That's not an answer, Beau."

"Best I can do, ma'am."

"You seem to be taken with the works of the playwright, Mr. Shakespeare."

"I enjoy his work, and have more than a passing knowledge of it."

"Do you recall the line, above all to your own self be true."

"Actually the line is 'this above all: to thine own self be true."

"Shouldn't you be?"

"Ma'am?"

"True to yourself, and true to me, who's treated you like a long lost brother."

I have to clear my throat with that, as it's true as a compass points north. "You have done that, ma'am, and I appreciate it."

"So, Beau, be true to me." Her tone was earnest and direct, and it made my mouth go a little dry.

I answer carefully. "Would I be able, without compromising my friend, Mr. Pettigrew, I would do so. I can only say this, ma'am . . . I have no idea where Mr. Pettigrew might have slept last night, and that's the God's honest truth."

She seems exasperated, and shakes her head, seemingly in some disgust. "You dance like a trained bear, Mr. Boone. We may have to talk some more before I determine what's to become of you, of Mr. Pettigrew, and of this place I've worked so hard to bring to some success. I'm suddenly very tired of the whole affair. . . ."

"Ma'am," I say, and tip my hat. "I have a date for lunch, so if you don't mind I'll return to my room and get freshened up."

She smiles for the first time. "A date? Why I think that's fine. With one of our girls, or?"

I return the smile, if a little sheepishly. "No, ma'am. With a new friend, Mrs. Traintor. We're to discuss the very subject you brought up . . . the bard. It seems she was a teacher of English literature before becoming a shop keeper."

"She's a fine woman. She's always treated

me fairly and with respect. More than I can say for a few of the other women in Nemesis. Stay a while if you'd like. We won't be getting busy until late in the afternoon."

"Thank you," I say, tip my hat again, and head for the doors feeling like a coward retreating before General Lee's Confederate charge at Gettysburg.

She stops me as I put a hand on one of the batwings, calling out, "Beau, Pet doesn't deserve a friend like you."

I smile, wanly, but a smile, then give her another line. " 'And it must follow, as the night the day, thou canst not then be false to any man.' "

She nods, then adds, as with inquiry, "I presume 'man' he used in the biblical collective sense, not the gender sense, including women in the term."

"I'd suppose," I say, tip my hat again, and hurry out before my feet are again held to the fire.


Mrs. Traintor was exactly on time, a trait I admire in a person.

It has always seemed to me that being habitually late is thinking you and your time more important than the other person's. I seat her at a nice table in front of a window, in fact the same table Mr. Pettigrew and I had shared after the affair in the street that resulted in the loss of three men's lives.

I offer Mrs. Traintor a glass of wine, but she refuses but without affront, and both of us settle on sweet tea.

I find myself enthralled by Jessie Traintor, who invites me to call her by her first name. We talk for over an hour over oyster stew, oysters fresh off the transcontinental, and fresh rolls, then over a tumbler of brandy, a treat she says I've introduced her to as she claims she'd never tasted the nectar and in fact, hasn't had alcohol cross her lips since her husband's demise. I'm also happy to note that the mention of him in regards to alcohol was the only time a recollection was made of Mr. Traintor.

Strangely enough, the bard is never mentioned during our prolonged lunch, so I take the opportunity to mention that fact, and to make another date for a Sunday picnic — her son included — in order to broach that subject at some length. She agrees, and after walking her back to her store, I cover the rest of the way to the Angel on light feet whistling a happy tune.

I push through the batwings to find Mr. Pettigrew nowhere in sight, and Miss Alice and Martha Ann nose to nose, and they aren't talking about the weather.

Miss Alice notices my entry, or I would beat a hasty retreat. She waves me over and I find myself standing, front and center, before her. Her yellow eyes are no longer spitting shards of ice, but rather lightning bolts.

Before she can speak, five burly men wearing badges push though the batwings. I cannot decide, am I saved, or sacrificed?

As the bard proclaimed, when sorrows come, they come not single spies, but in battalions.

# CHAPTER THIRTEEN

The morning train brought oysters from the west; the afternoon lawmen from the east.

Without the courtesy of extending his hand, a man with a handlebar mustache to equal that of Mr. Pettigrew crosses the room to where I stand, and introduces himself. "I'm United States Marshal Josiah McCallister, and these are my deputies. You are?"

"Beau Boone," I answer, and he ignores my extended hand. It is all I can do not to proclaim him a rude son of a bitch then and there, but under the circumstance, think better of it.

"Has anyone here seen Marshal Keller? He was due to meet us at the station."

Miss Alice rises and moves up beside me. "If you gentlemen are here for a drink, there's the bar. I have not seen Marshal Keller . . . anyone else?" She surveys the room and gets only a shake of the head from Horace, Martha Ann, and myself.

"Then, gentlemen, either have a drink or take your leave. This is not the town meeting hall, but rather a saloon."

She has not made a friend of Marshal McCallister, as his jaw knots and his eyes narrow as he inquires, "And a man named Pettigrew, is he near at hand?"

"Normally Mr. Pettigrew is here at this time of day. However, he was called away on other business. You boys have a drink and I imagine he'll be along, if you'd like to wait and spread a little silver on the bar."

The marshal turns as if to leave, but his move is trumped by his men who seem to think it a fine idea to pass a little money across the bar. Even in the eyes of adversity, Miss Alice knows how turn a dollar, and to ply for a little information. As the marshal heads for the bar, she speaks up. "Marshal, join me here at my table and I'll stand you to three fingers of good whiskey."

He stops short, eyes his men for a moment, then this very attractive woman, and moves to join her.

She extends her hand, and he takes it, then sits. "You the proprietor here, miss?"

"It's Miss Alice. And yes, this is my place."

"Alice Hockstead, came here from Denver?"

She's a bit taken aback. "Yes, and came

here after paying what you'd call my debt to society and I'd call a raw deal, but that's neither here nor there."

"You killed a man in Oro City . . . an unarmed man, shot him down like a dog rumor says, and I guess more to the point, a jury said. Had you not been a woman, you would have hanged, rather you got a lousy two years."

"Had there been any witnesses other than his employees, I would have been set free . . . but like I said, that's all old news and my so-called debt is paid. Men should not lay their hands on a woman in anger. And for your information a man . . . who is so much stronger than a woman . . . needs no weapons to have his way with her."

He gives her a smirk, but drops it.

Then, his voice gets an edge. "So, who killed Judge Rankin?"

"That's why you're here?"

"Did you think killing a federal judge would go unnoticed?"

She shrugs. "Some two bit thief, I imagine. No witnesses, and his purse was missing, or so Marshal Keller reported."

He looks over at me. "Boone, as I hear it you and this Pettigrew were about to be indicted for murder. You and Pettigrew had plenty of motive."

"No murder, marshal. Fair fight, the two of us against five if you can call that fair, them with the five, us with the measly two, and it wasn't us went looking for them. They came hunting, we were just better shots."

"Humph," he says, "and faster . . . who fired first?" and turns his attention back to Miss Alice without getting an answer, obviously not expecting one. He is not looking at her like she's some wanted woman, but rather like she's a juicy pork chop and he's starving. No matter what he's saying, his eyes give him away.

They've left me standing like a knot on a log, so I begin to ease away toward my stool at the end of the bar. Miss Alice, in a tone sharp as a witch's tongue, snaps at me, "Boone, bring the Marshal a bottle of our finest, and a bowl of those goobers."

Being mannerly, even though I somewhat resent the tone, I reply, "Yes, ma'am." And do so along with a couple of newly shined glasses, and only then retreat to my position, careful not to pick up the scattergun leaning nearby. Five burly lawmen seem enough to keep the peace in the Angel, and it doesn't seem wise to antagonize, particularly when I've been nearly accused of the murder of a federal judge.

From my position facing the front of the saloon, and with the four deputy marshals at the bar and the marshal with his back to the door, I'm the only one to see Mr. Pettigrew walk up to the doors, but he peers inside, does a pirouette to rival the best toe dancer, and is as quickly gone. It appears he won't be putting in his normal appearance at the Angel this evening.

It's almost two hours, and near the time the Angel will be beginning to fill up with patrons, when Territorial Marshal Ivan Petrovich Keller pushes through the batwings. He takes a seat with Miss Alice and Marshal McCallister, and as the level of voices are rising, with the four marshals now into their third or fourth whiskey, I can no longer hear the conversation at the table.

As the place begins to fill up with the evening trade, Martha Ann sidles over next to me. "I done got my titty in a wringer," she says.

"Caught between a rock and a hard spot," I say, sympathizing. "What did you tell her?"

"I told her the truth. The boss wanted a little poke, and I obliged. What was I to do?"

"A little poke?" I couldn't help but ask.

"Half the damn night, fact was."

"And Miss Alice has never asked you to stay away from Mr. Pettigrew."

"Subject never came up. Wasn't my place to turn him down."

"Well, unless he asked you to lie and you felt your loyalty was to him, you did exactly the right thing . . . but the fact is, Miss Alice pays you, not Mr. Pettigrew, even though he acts like the boss around here . . . so you owe her the truth."

She shrugs. "Well, she got it, and didn't much like it, but she didn't boot me out so I guess she don't think I'm to blame." Then Martha Ann leans over and gives me a peck on the cheek, and as quickly returns, joining Blossom, hobnobbing with the men beginning to fill the place.

Another half hour passes before the confab at the table breaks up, and Miss Alice disappears out the rear door. Marshal McCallister walks straight to my end of the bar and stops a pace away. "You, sir, will appear at the Olympic in the morning promptly at ten to meet with Judge Hollis Procter and answer some questions. Miss Hockstead will be there as well. Understand, or do I have to find a place to lock you up for the night?"

"Why wouldn't I be willing to appear, marshal? I've got nothing to hide, nor does Mr. Pettigrew."

"The judge will be the judge of that, Boone. Just be there so I don't have to run you down and drag you in."

I don't bother to comment on that, and just give him a concise nod. Then I give him a bit of a smirk. "Marshal, there's a bit of peanut in that mop on your upper lip. Doesn't look lawman like."

He huffs a bit, brushing the mustache with splayed fingers. Then he gives me a glower, obviously not appreciating my concern with his grooming.

"In the morning," he repeats, and I nod again, then he continues, his brow furrowing. "You sure you don't know where to find Pettigrew?"

"I ain't his keeper," I say, again giving him as hard a look as I can muster, but he can see I'm amused, and it irritates him.

He rounds up his men and they head out. So a new judge has come in on the train along with the five U. S. Marshals. It's going to be an interesting time in old Nemesis tomorrow . . . in fact, as the Chinese say, may you live in interesting times.

I hope these times don't get too damned interesting.

# CHAPTER FOURTEEN

Mr. Pettigrew is nothing if not brazen.

He is not laying low in the cottage he shares with Miss Alice, but rather I find him snoring away in my bed in my garret room on top the Olympic with five marshals and a federal judge in the rooms on the second floor. The best place to hide, if he is hiding, is oft times under the wing of those hunting you.

I make myself a pallet on the floor next to the bed, and join him snoring away in moments.

He shakes me awake well before I've had my normal seven hours.

"So, what's the story on all those badges in the Angel last night?" he asks as I sit up and rub the sleep out of my eyes.

I yawn and stretch and clear my head before I answer. "You best be worried about a woman who spits and growls every time she speaks your name."

"Alice? Hell, she'll get over it. It ain't the first time I've been in my cups and shoved a round-heels over on her backside for a poke."

"She doesn't look like a woman who'll get over it to me," I say.

"Well, fact is, the last time it happened I swore it would be the last time. But she'll get over it. She knows a hard pecker's got no restraint, particularly after it's been pissin' a quart or so of rotgut."

"Then why didn't you head for the cottage last night? You crawled into my sack cause you thought you'd be welcome at home?"

"Don't badger me, Boone. You ain't my beloved." He's stroking his mustache and I know he's getting irritated.

"Not sure you got one anymore, but it's not my business." It's time to change the subject. "This U. S. Marshal, who barged into the Angel yesterday along with four of his men has ordered me, and Miss Alice, to come to the dinning room downstairs at ten this morning to answer questions from the new territorial judge. They tried to find you, so I was told, to order your appearance. You gonna show up?"

As is his habit, he's stroking that handlebar mustache, then snaps, "Hell no, I'm getting tired of this whole mess. Wilkenson and his boys want my hide to tack on the barn wall along with other hunting trophies. Alice would offer it up, so it seems — piss poor timing me giving Martha Ann a little poke — and some damn fools think I had something to do with putting Judge Rankin toes up —"

"Did you?"

He gives me a long hard stare, and his speed stroking the mustache increases ten fold . . . then he stops and offers, "Well, Beau Boone, if I did it was to your advantage as he was in bed with Wilkenson and it was likely we'd both be doing the hangman's jig had he had his way."

"So, is that an answer?"

The furrows in his brow are deep enough to have been plowed by a mule drawn. Finally, he sighs deeply. "Do you really want to know?"

Now it's my turn to give him a long hard stare. But it's a valid question, and I answer it truthfully. "Fact is, come to think on it, I don't want to know."

"Good, then go tell the new judge everything you know, 'cause you don't know a damn thing."

He clears his throat, then looks at me with a little reticence, sighs again, and continues.

"The fact is, I do care for Alice, and I did loan her the money to go into business. It was one hundred percent my money that went to buy the Angel. But there is no note, it was between she and I. And it has come to me, I die, either from Wilkenson and his bunch or the judge and his, and she don't have to pay up. Ironic isn't it. That poke I could'a bought for a dollar, and got for free, may just cost me three thousand."

"It's often attributed to the bard, but it was actually from a play written by a fella named Congrove or Congreve —"

"What's that?"

"Hell hath no fury like a woman scorned."

"No truer words. . . ."

"Where are you going to be?"

"Not that you need to know, but I'm gonna slip out of here and head for the cottage before Alice comes to work, and see if she's calmed down and wants to make peace."

"Don't be holding your breath," I say, and get to my feet and take the two steps to my bone white pitcher and bowl and pour some water so I can wash up and slick down my hair, and use a finger to shine my teeth with the bicarbonate of soda I keep there for the purpose.

"Don't use all that," Mr. Pettigrew says,

as it seems he might want to be on his best for his upcoming meeting with Miss Alice, if he can get there without being detained by the U. S. Marshals.

He leaves, wanting to get out of the hotel before others are scurrying about . . . particularly a bevy of U. S. Marshals.

Deciding I want to at least look presentable, I hobble down two flights of stairs to the kitchen, fill my pitcher with hot water, hobble back up, and strop my razor, soap up, and shave.

Spit shined and hair slicked, I'm having breakfast an hour later in the dining room when the marshals appear, just before eight a.m. With them is a tall man with silver gray pork chop sideburns, in a fancy black frock coat and a high hat. Had he a more predominant proboscis I might have mistaken him for our recent head of state — of course that gentleman being dead convinces me otherwise — but this man's nose is actually pugged and appears to have been rearranged by someone who took umbrage at one of his rulings. It's damned crooked, in fact. He does, however, have some length to his ears and is a bit long in the tooth, all testifying that he's no neophyte in the Church of Law. And I would guess him less than six feet in height, and Mr. Lincoln was over that, if the papers can be believed.

McCallister nods at me, but they take a table across the room. I'm finished with my ham and eggs, biscuits and blackberry jam, and about finished with the Leslie's Weekly, when Miss Alice enters the room. She gives Marshal McCallister a nod, but comes and joins me at my table. I rise and seat her, as a gentleman should.

After Aggie Papadopolous pours Miss Alice a cup of coffee, and excuses himself to bring her the bowl of porridge with a dollop of honey she's ordered, she reaches over the table and covers one of my hands with hers. "I'm sorry, Beau. You got caught up in Pet's wrongdoing and I put you square on the spot. It was unfair of me. I also owe Martha Ann an apology and she'll get it when she comes in this afternoon. She was merely doing what she's paid to do. Am I forgiven?"

"Nothing to forgive. You asked honest questions."

"And you gave honest answers."

I did not ask if that was a question, hoping the subject was dropped.

Rather, I asked, "Will Mr. Pettigrew be here for this inquisition?"

"Between you and I and this salt and pepper shaker, I'd be very surprised. He's not convinced that Wilkenson is not in bed with this new judge as well. Wilkenson has proven to be a land based octopus, with tentacles into business and territorial government; he's spread a portion of the gold from his mine far and wide. Until Wilkenson is proven to have no undue influence over this judge, Pet'll remain difficult to find."

And I can't help but ask, "And you and Mr. Pettigrew have . . . shall I say, have made peace?"

"A cease fire, at least."

That makes me smile.

"That pleases you?" she asks.

"Peace would be better, but a cease fire I understand. Let's get these marshals out of our hair, hopefully after this discussion today . . . then maybe things can get back to normal."

She laughs a little sardonically. "With Pet shooting down Wilkenson's boy, I don't think there'll ever be a 'normal' again. Not to speak of his betrayal. . . ."

"Marshals first, then *que sera sera.*"

Just as I finish my sentence, Marshal McCallister appears at tableside.

"Since you two are here, and we've all finished our breakfast, the judge would like to get things underway."

126

Miss Alice bats her eyes at him. "I have yet to be served, thank you, marshal. However, Mr. Boone is finished."

I rise, fold up my napkin, and ask, "If you'll excuse me, Miss Alice, I'll tell him everything I know in about one minute. They'll have to wait for you to finish your porridge unless they have others to talk with."

# CHAPTER FIFTEEN

Just as I rise, I see Wilkenson and his remaining four boys, at least they all look to be related, enter the dining room, along with Simon Chastaine, the manager of the bank. Just behind them is Marshal Pete Keller, and behind him is Andy McBride, the barber.

It appears to be a regular town meeting.

We retire to a side room which has three tables dragged together surrounded by a dozen chairs; it's off the main dining room and has double doors with acid-etched glass panels — a scene of European stags — separating it from the main room, and royal purple drapes at the windows. The carpet is forest green with garlands of purple flowers. It's a regal room befitting a serious meeting.

Judge Procter is at the head of the table and I'm directed to the foot. There is another young lady present, one I've seen on the street in Nemesis, but do not know. She has paper and pen, I presume to record the proceedings.

To my surprise, I'm sworn in by Marshal McCallister, hand on the Bible, before I take my seat.

"You understand these proceedings?" the judge asks.

"I understand I'm sworn and obliged to tell the truth, and the truth is I don't know a damned thing. Can I go now?"

That actually brings a smile to the judge's face and a scowl from McCallister.

"This in an inquest, for the purpose of determining who, if anyone, needs to go to trial in this fair city of yours. We're going to cover a number of things, including the shooting you were involved in, and the subsequent murder of Judge Rankin. You'll be here a while, Mr. Boone," the judge says, after he quits chuckling.

"I don't have to be at work until this afternoon," I offer, and he smiles again.

He spends nearly an hour raking me over the coals. I swear, by the time he's finished he knows more about me than I know about myself. He seems satisfied when I'm finally excused.

"Don't leave town," McCallister instructs, as I nod as I head out the door.

Wilkenson and his three sons are gathered at a circular dining room table playing cards as I pass. The old man calls out to me. "You know, Boone, I hold you equally responsible for my son's murder."

That stops me short and I hobble up between two of his boys and lean over the table, as much in his face as I can get with the round table between us. "Wilkenson, I hadn't even been inside that saloon when your son came flying out the door and knocked me into the mud. The next time I saw him, he was charging Mr. Pettigrew with a Winchester in hand, cocking it and aiming to send him to hell. I had nothing to do with his shooting, but I would have shot him under the same circumstance . . . and anybody would, including you and any of these louts."

That didn't even slow him down. "And you killed my men, MacIntosh, McWilliams, and the mex, Sanchez. You got hands just as dirty as that lowdown Pettigrew, and you'll pay for that as well."

"They came shootin' and lead was knocking chunks out of the woodwork all around my head, so I guess I was to ask them to palaver? You're a damn fool, Wilkenson, if you think you would have done anything different than what Pettigrew and I did."

The two sons flanking me both rise, each a half-head taller than I, hands knotted into fists at their sides, and I prudently back away from the table, but I'm still talking. "I guess, if you're saying you're gonna shoot me down, then the next time I see any Wilkenson, I should start shooting first and ask questions later?"

I'm continuing to back toward the door as I speak. At a nearby table three of McCallister's deputies are on their feet, and I'm interrupted.

The voice obviously directs his first comments to the Wilkensons. "You all sit back down," then turns on me, "and you, Boone, you get on out of here." I give my back to the table and realize it's coming from one of the deputies. I tip my hat to him, spin on my heel, and head for the door.

As soon as I enter the Angel, Horace waves me over to the bar, and leans over and informs me in a low tone, "Pettigrew wants to see you. He's at the cottage."

"Tell Miss Alice where I've gone when she gets in." I hurry out and head for the cottage, only I go the other way down the street to begin with, then work my way across the street and behind that row of buildings, then head back to the old burned out church and the cottage, making sure I'm not being watched.

I slip up to the back door and give it a rap.

"Come on in, Beau," he shouts.

To my surprise, he has on one of Miss Alice's lace trimmed aprons and is at the stove, stirring a pot of soup. I'd never thought of him as domestic.

"You have lunch yet?" he asks.

"Had a big breakfast," I say, not really wanting to be dining with him when a bevy of marshals burst in the door.

He ladles himself a bowl full, tears a chunk off a loaf of bread, pours himself a mug of buttermilk, and takes a seat. I sit on the edge of my chair across from him.

Between bites, buttermilk coloring his mustache, he offers in a casual tone, "We've got to kill that rich son of a bitch, Wilkenson."

# CHAPTER SIXTEEN

At first I'm taken aback, but as he chews I, truthfully, can see the logic in what he says. Wilkenson won't quit until we're toes up, and the only way to make it stop is for him, and probably his kin, to be dead.

That still, however, doesn't solve the problem of the death of a federal judge, which has resulted in another judge and five federal marshals digging into every aspect of life in Nemesis, as well as the man who's sitting across from me being one who's dodging them and is probably the culprit in the judge's murder. That has yet to be established, and as I've already decided, I don't want to know.

I can't help but be somewhat facetious, and ask, "So, you think we can find Wilkenson drunk and slit his throat in an alley and make it look like some petty thief did the job."

He gives me a bit of a glare, but ignores

my cynicism. "I was thinking about finding him with only one or two of those dolts he calls sons, and goading him into a fight."

"Well, hell, Mr. Pettigrew, he's over in the hotel waiting to try and get us hung this very minute. Why not go over there and goad the old boy?" He knows I'm digging him, and doesn't much like it.

"Are you mad at me, Boone? You think I did Miss Alice wrong, don't you? You may be looking up to her just a little too much."

"She's a fine lady —"

"She's a murderer and a whore and has yet to pay her debt to me, so she's a welsher as well."

That stopped me cold, and to be truthful, made me a little angry. "You shouldn't talk like that, Pettigrew."

"And you should open your eyes and take a look around. She hired you at my request, even though you looked like something the cat just buried. But she is smart enough to know that some ol' boy with only half a leg is going to work extra hard to prove he's as good or better than the next fellow. And you've proven yourself to be. But now it's come down to who's better than the next fellow, and Wilkenson is the next fellow. He has his way and the crows will be picking at your eyes and mine. We need to find a good high spot between here and that mine of his, and when he's riding home, you need to borrow my 45/70 and put an ounce of lead in his chest, and into any who ride with him. You've got a good horse . . . that I gave you, by the by. He'll carry you clean out of the territory. Only when Wilkenson is feeding the worms will we have some peace in this town."

"And what are you doing all this time? While I'm murdering an upstanding citizen out on the road, then running to keep my neck from being stretched?"

"Why, I'll be in plain sight of half the town, taking care of business in the Angel."

"While I'm committing murder?"

"Yep. They expect me to be killing Wilkenson, so I need to be seen when it's being done. Remember, you were in the Angel when Judge Rankin met his maker. This'll make us even up."

"So you did slit Judge Rankin's throat." I get up and plant my cane with some strength. "It's not going to happen that way, Mr. 'P.' The fact is, I don't do murder. I don't mind spilling blood if need be, and the cause requires, but I don't do murder. You enjoy your lunch. I'm going back to work."

With that, I make my way to the back

door, and exit. Neither of us bothering with goodbye.

As I'm gimping my way back to the Angel, I can't help but think of another of the bard's best: "And thus I clothe my naked villainy with old odd ends, stol'n forth of holy writ; and seem a saint, when most I play the devil."

I owe Mr. Pettigrew, but there's a limit. . . .

Miss Alice is at her corner table, pince-nez glasses on, working on her journals when I enter. I head straight for her table and take a seat without being invited. "How'd it go with Judge Procter?" I ask.

"Fine as wine. Fact is, I had nothing to tell. You can't get blood out of the proverbial turnip." I give her a slight smile, then turn deadly serious. "Pettigrew tells me you murdered someone? He wants me to do the same. Is it something you'd recommend?"

Her pretty yellow eyes widen a bit. Then, with steady conviction, she launches into the story. "I killed a man in Oro City, a man who had his hands on my throat and didn't know I had a two barrel derringer in my reticule. Two of his employees, my co-workers, were in the room and know exactly what happened. He was what is known as a pillar of the community and was a deacon in the church, but in fact he was a lying four-flusher who cheated at everything he did, including on his wife . . . and took umbrage when his new lady friend . . . me . . . decided to leave town for greener pastures. He took a week to die as I shot him in the stomach, and every day he lived and with every moan the town got more angry. It only took them two days after he passed to find me guilty of murder and sentence me to hang in front of a blacksmith who the town appointed as judge, who knew about as much about the law as I know about banging out door hinges."

She takes a deep breath before continuing. I'm a bit fascinated, but don't say a word. I want her to spill the whole story.

"Luckily, a real judge in Denver commuted my death sentence before they could get a scaffold built, and reduced my sentence to five years, then when one of the employees who'd testified against me recanted, reduced my sentence again to three years and I was out in two, . . . but two years as one of three women in a men's prison, where I worked in the kitchen and infirmary in the day and was taken advantage of by a fat warden in the night, was pure hell. I don't imagine you've ever had a fat man wallow on you like a rutting hog? I should never have been there in the first instance."

"You don't owe me an explanation," I manage.

"You got it anyway. What does Pet want you to do?"

"Kill Wilkenson. Dry gulch him out on the road somewhere, and both his boys if I can get it done, then ride hell for leather into the next territory."

"Pet is good at doing you a favor, then wanting tenfold in return." Her eyes widen. "You may not have to wait," she says, looking over my shoulder. I turn, and see Wilkenson and his four boys enter through the batwings and head for the walnut bar.

That causes me to take a deep breath, and let it out in a sigh. Then I hobble for my stool at the end of the bar. There are only two customers in the place, at the far end of the bar nearest the doors. And they must sense trouble on its way, as they quickly exit. The Wilkensons take up the middle of the bar, and must be ready for some serious drinking as they order two full bottles of hooch.

Horace gives Miss Alice a look before he serves them, but she nods, and he goes ahead and places the bottles on the bar along with five glasses.

Each of the Wilkensons is well heeled, revolvers at their sides. I have made it to my scattergun, leaning under the bar, both barrels loaded with an ounce and a half of cut up nails, the barrel sawed off to fifteen inches which makes a pattern of about three feet at the fifteen foot distance to the nearest Wilkenson son. And they are all big barrel chested men, hard to miss should it come to that.

But two barrels and four men?

Then I remember the load in my cane handle, a single twenty five caliber barrel and load that I've never fired, but it's loaded with cartridge in place, and I may have to trust it.

While I'm contemplating my weaponry, Miss Alice rises and crosses the room to take up a position behind old man Wilkenson, who's the center of the Wilkenson clan with two sons on either side.

"Are you here looking for Mr. Pettigrew?" she asks the old man, who, hulking over his drink, answers, eyeing her from under bushy eyebrows in the mirror behind the bar, without the courtesy of bothering to turn and face her.

His voice is low and raspy. "Seems the judge decided not to indict anyone for either my son's murder or the judge's, or for the fight in the street. He decided that the judge was killed by a common thief, who's probably in San Francisco by now, and the rest of it self-defense."

"So, it's over?" she asks.

He begins to laugh, a small belly laugh that ends in a roar. His sons join in and a passerby would think the saloon the happiest of places. Only when he quits does he spin on the stool to face Miss Alice.

"I hear you got a couple of whores hereabouts?" he asks, and I can see that this is leading to no damn good.

"We have a couple of ladies of the night, if that's your inquiry."

"And you . . . you a whore?"

# CHAPTER SEVENTEEN

She gives him a tight smile and almost as quickly her back, obviously deciding discretion the better part of valor, and strides back to her table and books without replying. She adjusts her glasses, and goes back to her books.

He guffaws and turns back to face the bar.

Then I remember something and wave Horace over. He hurries to a place across the bar. I speak in little more than a whisper. "Put that coach gun of yours up on the bar."

"Pretty obvious, don't you think?" he asks, equally quiet.

"At the moment, obvious seems just fine." I give him a snarl to go along with my next comment. "I doubt if you're gonna use it as I've never seen you reach for it."

He moves back down the bar to where the second scattergun is racked underneath, and with some style removes it and keeps it low below the level of the bar, moving back my way. Wiping the bar with a towel as he comes and then using the towel to cover a good part of the weapon, he places it up against the wall at the end of the bar, butt facing me.

I find myself wishing I was out on that picnic with the Widow Traintor, even if I have to put up with her rather obnoxious son.

This is no place for a man who has limited mobility, not that I'll probably need mobility as they'll get five shots off to my one . . . but my one should take out at least two of them, God willing and the Humbolt River don't rise.

To my chagrin, two of the Wilkensons cross the room and take up a position at a Faro table — my hopes of them being bunched up fade — and one of them yells to Miss Alice, "You gonna deal, whore, or are you just around for some kind of sad, old, decoration."

Miss Alice must be in her early thirties, hardly old. She rises and crosses the room to me, not to the table, and speaks low enough that they cannot hear. "I'm leaving now, Beau. I will see if I can find Mr. Pettigrew, or Marshal Keller, or McCallister, or someone. . . . Don't do anything foolish. You don't owe Pet a damn thing. Be very careful. . . ."

As she heads for the door, one of the Wilkenson sons at the faro table yells after her. "Hey, I got me a quarter if'n you got time to drop your drawers and grab yer ankles."

The Wilkensons all find that funny, and again the place rings with laughter. The heat is beginning to creep up my backbone, but anger is sometimes one's friend, and sometimes not. With the odds as they are, I know it's wise to keep my wits about me, but the hell of it is, anger is sometimes its own master.

The two who've crossed the room to the faro table were the ones between old man Wilkenson and my position. Knowing I should keep my mouth shut, I don't. "Caleb, isn't it?" I call out.

He turns slowly. "Caleb it is, not that you're welcome to use the familiar. Beau Boone, is it not?"

"It is. And these are all your sorry kin?"

"It only seems right you should know who's about to put you in the sod. This is Seth on my left, Caleb Junior on his. That's Jed and Jacob over at the faro table, fixin to waste a quarter dollar on that whore owns this place."

"And the one that was such a piss poor shot . . . that was Rosco, right?"

I can see him anger, but he keeps his badger caged, at least for the moment.

"The one Pettigrew murdered, that was Rosco. Had he been sober, Pettigrew, and probably you, would have been dead men."

Had I any brains, I'd keep them talking, hoping that Miss Alice might bring some help. But it seems I have trouble in the brain department.

"So, which one of your boys is the ugliest, in your opinion?"

One of the two at the faro table starts across the room, looking as if he might want to rip my head off. The scattergun is hanging loosely in my right hand, down along the face of the bar, my cane is in my left, and as the big man comes, I raise the cane. "You Jed or Jacob?"

"Jed, asshole."

"Jed Asshole. That's an interesting name. I believe your father is going to be of no help with my quandary, so I have to make up my own mind, and I believe I have. You are undoubtedly the ugliest Wilkenson, now that butt-ugly Rosco has met his maker."

He steps close enough that I have the tip of the cane in his chest, he growls like a grizzly and tries to rip it out of the my hand, and to his surprise all he accomplishes is stripping the cane-scabbard off the blade.

His mouth drops open in astonishment, and surprised and suddenly frightened with the point of the blade now centered on his heart, he reaches for his sidearm as I drop the little metal trigger into place.

"Don't!" I yell at him, but he's already drawing his weapon. His eyes become saucers and his mouth widens with a silent scream as the butt of the cane explodes in his face and the little twenty five caliber ball takes him mid-chest, heart high, and he goes to his knees, gasping for breath, pumping blood out the tiny hole.

"Daddy!" he screams, and him a man of at least twenty-five years.

With my thumb across both, I cock the two barrels of the scattergun hanging in my other hand as I raise it to meet the other brother charging across the room from the faro table, and he only gets five feet before he's blown clean off his feet and back across the table . . . and it overturns with him riding it to the floor in a haze of red mist. I swing the muzzles down the bar and let loose the other barrel without looking to see if they are drawing weapons . . . there's no question in my mind they are.

The second barrel roars and I only then see that the two remaining brothers are standing side by side, one firing his weapon at me, one still drawing. The cut up square nails spin them both and they go to the floor, as the wall next to my head shatters with a big forty four slug.

The cloud of white powder smoke has occluded my vision.

Where's old man Wilkenson, flashes through my mind.

And only then do I see him rising from the floor where he either fell or dived when the first shot went off. He's up, revolver in hand, fire in his eyes, and I'm fresh out of loaded barrels. I grab for the coach gun on the bar and try and cock it as I bring it around, but something whacks me so hard I'm dislodged from the barstool and hit the ground flat on my belly, my ears ringing, and with the last thought of the acrid smell of gun smoke flooding my nostrils.

The lights go out.

# CHAPTER EIGHTEEN

This can't be hell as it's not hot enough.

There's a rosy haze as I pry open my eyes, which seem stuck shut. Then I focus on curtains covering a glass window, rose colored curtains, pulled tightly shut. I reach up, rub my chin, and run a finger over very dry lips. Whiskers, long enough to give under my inspection. Didn't I just shave this morning?

Suddenly a wet rag is rubbed over my lips, and I focus on a face.

"Blossom?" I ask.

"If it ain't Lazarus his very own self. I swear, I thought you dead as a salted cod fish for sure," she says, passing the wet rag over my brow.

And to be truthful, I'm wondering if I wouldn't be better off so. With each breath, I feel like someone is jamming a pitchfork in my chest.

"Where am I?" I ask, not recognizing my

surroundings.

"Mrs. Traintor has allowed us to use her extra room, as it seems it's one of the only places that Caleb Wilkenson is not looking for you. She may not have mentioned it, but Caleb Wilkenson has courted her from time to time. He came in her store inquiring about you. She's a fine liar and you should be thankful for it."

"Wilkenson's alive? Drink of water, please."

She fetches a glass and fills in from a pitcher on a bird's eye maple bureau with a lace trimmed coverlet lapping over the edges of its top.

It's ambrosia as I take a sip, although it pains me to even lift my head, and she answers my question. "He is alive, only scratched, but two of his boys are at the diggers, being planted tomorrow on a hill out near the mine. He dug up the one Pettigrew kilt and is reburying him out there. They got a regular cemetery going, thanks to you and the boss."

"The one I shot with the cane and the other one over at the faro table are dead?"

"Nope, the one you shot with that little bullet from the cane is hanging on with a hole in his chest from that tricky cane of yours, and another done lost an arm just below the elbow. You could'a kilt half the town with that scattergun. I never saw the like. . . ."

I start to rise, but the pain convinces me that the idea is a bad one. I gasp, and relax, waiting for the pain to wane. "How bad am I?"

"You took a bullet clean through your right side. Doc Peabody says it may have nicked a lung or even worse a bowel, and you could have a broke rib. He thinks you do. You don't want to start things to bleeding again. You done lost a washtub fulla blood."

"Blossom, no one carries a washtub full."

"Well, while the doc was working on you it looked like a washtub full."

"How come Wilkenson didn't finish me off?" I ask, my voice raspy and fading.

"All those U. S. marshals come busting in just as you hit the floor. Besides, Wilkenson thought you was already done for . . . so did everyone else."

"Where's Mrs. Traintor?"

"Running the store. I been watching you during her work time, and making two dollars a day from Miss Alice. It's like a vacation to me."

"Glad you're enjoying yourself."

I'm finding it difficult to continue to speak

as my throat hurts so badly, probably from being dry for so long.

"Miss Alice told the Wilkenson bunch and Marshal Keller that she put you on the train, and she paid Charley Snodgrass a ten dollar gold piece to swear to it . . . but Wilkenson don't seem to believe and he's hunting you none-the-less. But I hear he quit lookin' and headed back to that gold mine of his."

"And Mr. Pettigrew?" I rasp.

"He did get on the train, heading west. He and Miss Alice had it out and he cleaned out her little safe and the tills, and hotfooted it out of town. Which was fine, as Miss Alice said he was the one who escorted you on the train, so it made a fine story."

"How long will I be laid up?"

"Doc says at least two weeks in bed —"

"How long have I been here," I ask in a whisper again rubbing the stubble on my chin.

"That first night and three more days. It's about time for Mrs. Traintor to get home. She comes in just a little after six."

I reach out and take her hand. "Thank you, Blossom. I'm sure I'm a lousy patient."

"No trouble at all, Beau Boone. No trouble."

She heads for the door at the same time

as the Traintor boy, Alex, sticks his head in.

"He's awake," he says, and walks to the foot of the bed. He's looking somewhat amazed. "I thought you was a dead one for sure."

"Thanks, Alex."

He smiles sheepishly. "I don't mean I hoped you was dead, just thought you was a goner."

I give him a smile. "Too damn ugly to kill easy."

He gets an excited look. "Tell me about the gunfight. You kilt two of those owlhoots, and blowed the arm off another. I knew them from the store and they were big and looked tough as bull leather. How'd you do it?"

Blossom puts a hand in his chest and shoves him out the door. "He just woke up from being half dead, Alex. You run along . . . and remember, Mr. Boone ain't here. I got to hunt down the doc as soon as your mom shows up. He wanted to know when Mr. Boone awoke . . . if'n he did wake up, and he done did."

"Tomorrow," I call after Alex, and he waves as Blossom shoves him out the door.

"He's excited," she says. "I hope he don't spout it all over town about you being here. His mama said she'd send him away to boarding school, he said a word, but you know boys. Never been one who could keep his lip buttoned, particularly when it comes to girls."

It sounds to me like Miss Blossom had some boy telling tales about her, but I don't ask. "I don't imagine there might be some soup on the fire. A half cup would suit me fine."

"I'll see what I can do."

I do manage to get down a few sips of chicken soup and about the time I decide I can't get another sip down, Jessie Traintor knocks on the door jamb and peeks her head in, smiling, and I'd believe her an angel had I not already been told I was still among the living.

"You don't know how happy I am to see your eyes open," she says.

"Everything looks good from this side of the eyelids as well."

"And you haven't lost your sense of humor."

"Lost some blood, lost a chunk of my side, lost a bunch of self-confidence, but I'll be damned if I lost my sense of humor. I owe you, Mrs. Traintor."

"Any Christian woman would have done the same."

"I doubt that. There's some more than

Christian charity when there's risk involved." I close my eyes for a moment; seems I'm flat worn out.

"You rest now. You need the bed pan?"

I know my face has turned beet red. I guess these ladies have been tending to all my needs.

"No . . . no, ma'am. I'll be on my feet by tomorrow and can take care of myself."

"You'll be in bed for a week at least, so get used to it, mister. Now, you want the bedpan?"

I'm happy to say that for the next week, other than passing a little water, my requirements are minimum. By the seventh day, I'm on my feet and, finally able to eat solid food, and able to use the thunderpot without the embarrassment of a lady overlooking my necessaries. Mrs. Traintor, Blossom, and the formerly smart alec son, Alex, do an admirable job bringing me back to semi-normal, although it will be some time before I'm dancing a one legged polka.

Doc Peabody is pleased with my progress, and reports that the Wilkenson boy, Jed, who I believe I'd shot through the heart, is recovering nicely. Seems the little cartridge only penetrated an inch into his chest, severing some minor vein or artery, as he had on a heavy coat and the charge must have been poorly loaded. The one losing his forearm was Caleb Junior, and Jacob and Seth were the ones who expired. It seems it was Caleb Junior's right hand, his gun hand, so with luck he's out of the running for a while as an adversary, at least until he gets some practice with the left. Of course Wilkenson can hire two dozen shooters, should he find the need. If he's already done so, I'm sure he's sent them to San Francisco to run us down. That makes me smile, as it seems Miss Alice has engineered a fine ruse.

In the last few weeks Wilkenson has lost three of his five sons and the arm of another. I would hope him to be discouraged . . . but doubt it.

I spend another week holed up at the Traintor house, and find Mrs. Traintor to be fine company, and discover her to be a respectable cribbage player. Wilkenson has returned to his mine, fifteen miles out of town. Blossom has stopped coming as I'm able to take care of myself during the day, along with some help from Alex . . . who's gained an obvious respect for his peg-legged guest as he's impressed with my dispatching the Wilkenson boys. And he's much more respectful of his ma, at least when I'm in earshot. I spend a good deal of time trying to impress upon him that killing is a sin and that had I not had the job I had, I would never have engaged in the pastime. I find him hard to convince, as he seems to think there some glory in the endeavor. Miss Alice has not found time to visit with me at all; however she did pay Blossom to care for me, and that's something.

I'm running out of excuses to go back to work, and after Mrs. Traintor leaves for the general store, decide it's time for me to get back in the swing of things. If I leave without her presence, I'll not have to argue my way out. I compose a note expressing my everlasting indebtedness and the hope to take up the quest for a picnic, then dress, and hobble into the street. It's a block from the Traintor home to the main street, and I'm totally winded by the time I reach it and turn toward the Angel, another block ahead.

As luck would have it, the banker, Simon Chastaine, almost runs me over as he's leaving Andy McBride's tonsorial parlor. He stops, his jaw drops, and his eyes widen.

"What the hell . . . I thought you to be in San Francisco? Or on your way to China, which would be smarter."

"That was my twin brother, Beau. I'm Bob Boone."

"Bullshit, and you both one legged."

"You found me out, Chastaine. Mind getting out of my way so I can go to work?"

"Wilkenson will be happy to know you're back."

# CHAPTER NINETEEN

I take a deep breath and let it out slowly, then gird my loins and say in a low growl, "Tell him to come on. I'm ready to send him on to hell to meet up with his whelps."

The banker chuckles. "You look like a pile of horseshit that's been run over by a freight wagon."

I eye him with as tough a look as I can muster, which I'm sure isn't much in the way of tough. "Were I feeling better, I'd use this cane to make your back look as if you'd wrestled a cat-o'-nine-tails, but you're not worth the trouble of my further tiring myself. Go count your pennies, before I use this cane's blade to let the gas out of your puss-gut. Get out of my way; I've got to go to work."

He wisely steps out of reach of the cane. "Get your work done quick, Boone. Wilkenson will be happy to know where you are."

I hobble on as he moves away across the

street to the bank. I'm sure he'll dispatch a rider out to the Dead Horse Canyon mine before the morning is out.

I'm now wondering if I shouldn't take Mr. Pettigrew's suggestion and find myself a high lonely spot overlooking the road in from the mine, and send Wilkenson to his maker without risking my hide again . . . then realize it's only because I'm feeling weak and vulnerable. Murder still isn't in my bag of tricks, and a little weakness won't keep me from pulling the trigger on the blunderbuss scattergun at the saloon.

No one could be more surprised than this one-legged ex-artilleryman when I push through the batwings and see Mr. Pettigrew having coffee with Miss Alice, and both of them look equally surprised to see me.

"You're back," I offer to Mr. Pettigrew.

"Yep, I enjoyed San Francisco for over a week, then decided to come back here and look after my interests."

"You didn't get even when you cleaned out the safe and the till?"

"Five hundred and forty six dollars have been applied to Miss Alice's account, not that it's your affair." He's stroking his mustache again, eyeing me like a bull at a bastard calf, then sighs and suggests, "Beau, take a seat and have some coffee. You've had a hard couple of weeks."

"That I have." I turn to Miss Alice. "Do I still have a job?"

"You seem to be rather good at it, Beau. What kind of employer would I be to give the boot to a fella who spilled his blood for the good of the establishment. And I might add, protected my honor in the process. I thank you for that."

"Are those marshals gone?"

"They are," Mr. Pettigrew answers. "Soon as they were, Alice here sent me a wire."

Horace brings me a cup of coffee and his welcome and we shake hands. Then I turn to the two seated at the table. "I don't know what you two have between you, but it must be a powerful thing."

Both of them give me a smile. And Miss Alice offers, "Pure business, Mr. Boone, pure business. And, I might add, Mr. Pettigrew makes a fine pot of beans."

I shrug, and shake my head in wonderment just as Miss Penelope Ann comes through the back door carrying a tray of what I hope are cinnamon rolls, and prove to be. I have missed her baking, even if Mrs. Traintor is not only a fine specimen of the feminine gender, but a fine cook and hostess.

To be truthful, I have given thought, during my quiet times in her fine guest bed, of what it would be like to spend the rest of my days fathering her son, working behind the counter in her store, and being at her beck and call. Pipe dreams, I fear.

After I'm halfway through my roll, Mr. Pettigrew begins to chuckle, then inquires, "You could have waited, you know. Alice informed the marshals of the coming troubles, and she came to find me at the cottage. We all came a running."

"And you'd have come, even with the marshals here?"

"I would have come far enough to make sure you had some help."

"Pardon me, Mr. Pettigrew, but that's most likely hogwash. I saw you turn tail when you saw the marshals here earlier."

He doesn't take offense. "Hell, Boone, marshals weren't likely to shoot you down . . . and you didn't need any help as I hear it. Horace told me had you been a mite faster with that second scattergun, all of our problems would have been solved."

I nod. "However, they are not. I ran into the banker on my way here, and I imagine he's got a rider hightailing it out to Wilkenson's mine as we speak."

Mr. Pettigrew reaches over and pats me on the shoulder. "Well, hell, Beau. You're still a little stove up so I guess it's my turn this time."

Miss Alice rose and walked around to stand behind me, placing both hands on my shoulders. "Beau, I've kept your pay going while you've been recovering —"

"And you paid Blossom to take care of me. That was kind of you."

"I did, and was happy to do so. I owe you for two weeks. That's eighty dollars, and the fare to San Francisco is forty six. How about I pay you up and you take a ride on the Transcontinental before Wilkenson and half his mine employees come to town."

I smile a little wearily. "Fact is, I owe Mrs. Traintor for the room and board, and the fine care. I would arrive in San Francisco a gimpy ex-artilleryman with about enough money for a beer or two and a handful of goobers, just as I arrived in Nemesis. I think not. I may not have gained a lot since falling off the train car here, other than a hole in my side, but I have regained some self-respect, and some weapons to help me keep it, and I thank you both for that."

"How about that horse I gave you?" Mr. Pettigrew suggests. "You could ride out and just keep riding . . . with eighty dollars in your pocket."

"Which reminds me, I owe not only Mrs.

Traintor but Mr. Henderson at the livery for the care of my nag. I seem to be going in reverse here. I plan to pay my debts."

Miss Alice gives my shoulders a squeeze. "How about I make it an even hundred, Beau. It's the least I can do."

"Kind of you, but I got business here, Miss Alice. I can't be looking over my shoulder the rest of my life, and it was you who said that Wilkenson is like an octopus, with a long reach. No, I think we need to see this to the end, no matter how that comes about."

"Well," Mr. Pettigrew says, "it'll damn sure come about. Old man Wilkenson is a dogged bastard; like Sherman going though Georgia, he just keeps on coming."

I get to my feet. "Did Aggie keep my room for me?"

"Hell, Beau," Mr. Pettigrew says with a laugh, "he thinks you ran off to San Francisco with me. He might have packed up and stored your things if he's the good inn keeper I think he is."

"I had a few things there, so I'm gonna go check." I turn to Miss Alice. "I'll be back to take my shift."

"It's your funeral," she says.

"I hope not." I head out, leaving them to hobnob over coffee and cinnamon rolls, like two young sweethearts without a bit of water having passed under the bridge. It's a bit of a quandary to me, but then a good part of life seems to be.

My time recovering, my time spent with the Traintors, my quiet time thinking while healing, all has led me to believe I have more to live for than I'd thought when arriving in Nemesis. The loss of a piece of me seems now of much less consequence. But I wonder? Does the reckless abandon of not giving a damn if I live or die been a reason I've lived? Will I gain caution, thus becoming less of an effective threat to those wishing me harm, if I start thinking I have something to gain by living?

It would be a strange consequence should I die because I've decided I have something for which to live.

To prove to myself that I'm not only among the living, but wanting to do it in a proper manner, I hobble down to Lum Sing Ho's place and have myself a hot bath, then to Andy McBride's for a shave and a trim. One could say I was now ready to live in high style. Another might say I was fit to bury without causing the digger too much fret.

Life is surely strange.

# CHAPTER TWENTY

My room is still available, and I regain occupancy after negotiating at some length with Aggie Popadopolous over my vacating, as he says, without giving notice, and owing him for the time I spent at Mrs. Traintors . . . although I don't tell him that's where I've been domiciled this past two weeks. He wants to charge me, but my newly gained respect after facing down the Wilkenson clan seems to have some influence with Aggie. He doesn't want to cross me, and while we haggled, glanced a dozen times at my cane, as if it were a cobra. He admits that his place has not been full this past two weeks, and he wouldn't have rented the garret room none-the-less. He settles for one day extra.

He has stored my meager goods, which gains him some modicum of credit.

On my way back to take my shift at the Angel, I run into Charley Snodgrass, who runs the railroad station and operates the wire, which makes him the number one source of news for Nemesis and the surrounding area. After he expresses his admiration about the incident with the Wilkensons, he informs me that the Dead Horse Canyon mine has had a cave-in, and that Wilkenson and his boys will be engaged for some time. They have, however, hired another two dozen men, which makes them one of, if not the, largest employers in Northern Nevada Territory. Why couldn't I have picked an enemy too damn poor to buy ammunition?

I have trouble expressing my sympathy even though it seems a half dozen miners are missing in the cave-in — unfortunately no Wilkensons among them — and an extensive recovery effort is underway. I do not consider reporting out to Dead Horse Canyon and volunteering my assistance.

It seems I'll have a little more time to recover my strength — it still pains me to take a deep breath — and that Caleb Wilkenson will have some more time to quell his quest for revenge. Not that I think that likely.

The next three days at the Angel are inconsequential, and day by day, my strength is returning. Tonight will be a big night, as Saturday always is. I excuse myself before the evening rush begins, and hobble my way over to Trader Jake's General Store.

I'm happy to notice that the store is vacant other than Jessie Traintor, who's busy restocking shelves, and doesn't notice my entrance.

Being purposely quiet, I slip up behind her.

"I've brought you something," I say.

She's startled, and stands, placing a hand on her chest. "Beau Boone, how can you be so quiet, clunking along with that cane."

I smile and place an envelope on the counter. "I brought you a little something in the way of a thank you."

She reaches over and snatches up the envelope, opens it, and pulls out the three twenty dollar gold pieces I'd placed there.

"I can't take this, Beau. I enjoyed your company and it was the Christian thing to do."

"You don't run a rest home, nor a boarding house, Jessie. I want you to have that money as it'll only partly repay you for harboring me, at risk to yourself."

"Caleb Wilkenson wouldn't hurt me, no matter who I harbored. You want some tea?"

"Is Caleb a friend of yours?"

"Truth is," she says rather coyly, "he

wanted to be much more than that. But I put an end to it. He didn't seem the kind I wanted to have raise my son."

"Alex seems a fine boy, a little headstrong and large for his age, but even a seventeen hand horse can be taught better manners."

"Caleb's manners were a little on the rough side."

I decide to drop the subject. "I'd love to have some tea, but only if you'll take that little bit of reward for your kindness."

"Well, I won't, so I guess you don't get some tea. I will retain the three dollars you still owe for the cane."

"Come on, Jessie. It's only right you take it all."

"You force that money on me and I'll be insulted, Beau Boone. In fact I'm already insulted, as you promised to take me on a picnic, and have not shown your face around here since you skulked away without so much as a goodbye or howdy-do."

I laugh as I can see the humor in her eyes. "You're right, I did, but I knew you might try and hogtie me if I tried to leave while you were home."

She turns serious. "You've put yourself back in harm's way . . . again."

"Life goes on, Jessie. How about that picnic tomorrow or a week from tomorrow, if that's too little notice. You can bring Alex and we can take a buggy and head down by the Humbolt."

"That sounds fine, a week from Sunday as I'm engaged tomorrow . . . but only if you take this money back and don't think of paying me ever again." She makes change from her cash drawer, then drops the coins into my shirt pocket. Then she adds, "Alex is going fishing with his friends every Sunday after church for a while. We may see him down on the river."

I nod. "What time Sunday a week?"

"Noon. I'll fry up a chicken in the morning, and bake us an apple pie."

"And I'll go over to Hutchinson's and line up a buggy."

"Don't be late," she calls after me as I head out. "You could drop by between now and then for a cup."

"I'd like that, and will make a point to do so."

As every day goes by, I'm finding more reasons to love life, and think upon how close, and how many times, I'd almost ended it, or had it ended for me. And me a young buck with half a life left to live.

As I wander away, I do wonder what engagement she has that's keeping her from going on the picnic tomorrow. Could she still be seeing Wilkenson?

When I return to the Angel, Marshal Pete Keller and Mr. Pettigrew are leaning on the walnut bar, engaging in what appears to be a heated conversation. Mr. Pettigrew is stroking his mustache, a bad sign. Miss Alice is in her corner, studying her journals through her pince-nez glasses seeming unaware of the argument at the bar. Horace is as far down the end of the bar as he can get, obviously wanting no part of the conversation.

As I seem to be tarred with the same brush as Mr. Pettigrew, at least in the eyes of the law, I stride on over, my peg and cane making alternate clicks on the wood floor as I do so. Keeping Mr. Pettigrew between us, I join them, and wave Horace down. "Tall glass of water, please, Horace."

Both Mr. Pettigrew and Marshal Keller turn to face me. Keller remains silent; Pettigrew anything but. "This law dog still thinks I killed the judge, and that we should be under the gavel for that gunfight in the street."

I can't keep my mouth shut. "Marshal, who pays your salary?"

"Why, Nevada Territory. Why?"

"I'll be damned. The way you act I'd of thought it was Caleb Wilkenson."

I can see he doesn't cotton to that remark, as he's getting red in the face.

Finally, he sputters, "Boone, if you were a whole man, I'd whip you for that remark."

"Tell you what, marshal. I'm damn sure whole enough to give you a lesson. If it makes you feel better, I'll throw this peg away and Mr. Pettigrew here will tie your leg up ankle to thigh, and we'll have at it, equal up?"

Mr. Pettigrew starts to laugh at that, and I can't help but smile. Marshal Keller doesn't think it a bit amusing. He sputters again, "To hell with you. In fact, to hell with you both."

The smile fades from Mr. Pettigrew's face. "Pete, we've been friends for a long time. Three years or so . . . every since Alice and I came to town. I don't know why you've taken this dislike for me. But I've decided we're no longer friends —"

"We never were. You hoped to be, but we never were."

"Then do me a big favor, as it's beginning to rile me every time I see you coming. Don't come back in the Angel unless you've got official business."

He reddens even more. "I'm the marshal in this area. You can't tell me where to go and where not to go."

"Okay, I can't. . . ." Mr. Pettigrew closes the space between them until he's almost chest to chest with Keller. They're the same height, but Pettigrew is much thicker through the chest. "But I can shove that hogleg of yours so far up your backside that Doc Peabody will have to dig it out."

# Chapter Twenty-One

The two men are staring at each other, and I believe Mr. Pettigrew is getting truly angry. His jaw is beginning to knot and his fists are clinched, but it's Keller who breaks the silence.

"You pull iron on me, Pettigrew, and I'll put you in chains," Keller says, but his tone is weak.

"Pete, you must have those five marshals just outside, cause that's what it'll take to get me in chains."

"Well . . . well . . . I've got no cause or I by God would."

"Then if all we're gonna do is jaw, find someplace else to drink. I'm all talked out."

The marshal's still sputtering as he heads for the batwings, but Pettigrew stops him up short. "Keller, you owe fifty cents for the whiskey."

The marshal turns, and I'm wondering if he's not having some kind of attack, as his brow pops with moisture, and his jaw's so knotted it's a wonder his teeth aren't shattering. He digs a coin out of his pocket and throws it at . . . not to, but at, Horace.

Smashing through the batwings so hard they bang off the front walls, he's gone.

Mr. Pettigrew is smiling broadly. "Damned if that ain't the first time Keller's ever paid for a drink in here."

I shrug. "You do have a way of making the law spit and sputter. I hope that's the end of it."

"He was so mad because you hit the nail on the head. He is on the take from Wilkenson, just like half the law, politicians, and judges in this part of Nevada."

"Not Judge Procter. He couldn't have been more fair."

"The year is young, Mr. Boone. Wilkenson will get his tentacles in Procter as well, if all goes as normal."

I think on that for a moment, then offer, "I hope not. That hearing was not a trial, so double jeopardy doesn't apply. He could still bring us up on charges, should he change his mind or get new information . . . or should Wilkenson get to him."

"Wilkenson is our problem now. And we need to end it, and him."

"He's busy out at his mine with a cave-in.

And I'm in no shape to be trading gunshots with some lowlifes, and won't be for a while. Let things cool down. Besides, I got a date with a lovely lady."

"Tonight. You gotta work tonight."

"I'm going on a picnic."

"Tomorrow?"

"A week from tomorrow."

"Hell, that's a week away. Lots can happen in a week."

"Not this week, cause I've got a date a week hence. And I plan on keeping it. Fried chicken and new baked apple pie."

Pettigrew laughs out loud until the tears run down his cheeks. "Now that's rich, you not wanting any trouble cause you got a date in a week, and chicken and apple pie. And you sitting shotgun in a hell on wheels saloon." He chuckles some more, then gets a little more serious. "Let's hope the Wilkenson bunch isn't headed for town. Even though his sons are out of commission, he's got a half dozen guards and three or four dozen miners at his disposal. And it's Saturday night, and those boys usually want to howl."

"I don't want to wish those miners bad luck, but I hope he's still involved at that mine of his, and will be for months. However, I'll check my loads, and this time I'll have both scatterguns at hand."

"Don't kill any paying customers, if you can help it . . . unless their name is Wilkenson." He laughs aloud, and heads over to join Miss Alice, and like I said, I go to check my loads.

It's Friday, and the week, so far, is quiet. I've taken two opportunities this past week to visit Jessie Traintor for a cup of tea, and only two although I would have enjoyed doing so every day, but I don't want to make a pest of myself. I casually try and worm out of her why she couldn't have made the picnic the prior Sunday, a day on which she indicated she was "engaged." But she talks around it and I'm in no position to press the issue.

Mr. Pettigrew and Miss Alice alternate between looking at each other with doe eyes and looking as if they'd like to slit each other's throat. Seems something less than a healthy relationship to me, so I avoid joining them when they are both at the table. Of course, after the comments Mr. Pettigrew made about Miss Alice, a whore and a cheat if my memory serves me, I don't know how it could be a lasting, loving, relationship.

I, however, have seen no evidence of either

of those accusations.

She's made no accusations in regard to his actions, other than slipping and inferring that he was responsible for the judge's death. Which, of course, he was.

They've both been kind to me, so I'll try not to judge, and certainly not to take sides. It's becoming more and more obvious to me that I would be facing the hangman had Judge Rankin gone down the path Mr. Pettigrew felt him to be travelling . . . still, I can't condone murder.

More than once this week I've had the urge to take Miss Alice up on her offer to put me on a train to San Francisco, and if I weren't so looking forward to the opportunity to spend a day with Jessie Traintor, I'd probably be chugging over the Sierras right now on my way to a new life in San Francisco.

Instead, I'm working away in the Angel just as if a gaggle of shooters from the Dead Horse Canyon mine were not likely to show up to ventilate my hide as soon as their cave-in troubles are over.

Life goes on, and then it doesn't.

I'm thinking of leaving, and to my surprise, I'm not the only one. When I appear for my morning coffee and sweet roll, I'm joining only Miss Alice at the table nearest the batwing doors. Mr. Pettigrew is missing. To my concern, Miss Alice glances up from her journals and I can see she has a small cut under her eye and it's blackened a little.

"You trip and fall?" I ask.

"No, Boone, I didn't trip and fall, nor did I run into a door, nor did a mule kick me. Although I was struck by a jackass."

"Not Mr. Pettigrew?" My mouth is slightly agape.

"Enough said. I have a proposal for you."

"A proposal?"

"How would you like to buy the Angel?"

I laugh, then when she doesn't, get serious. "If you offered it to me for a hundred dollars I couldn't buy one of the mugs."

"Won't be quite that cheap. But I'll give you excellent terms."

"Like I said, Miss Alice, I can't afford a mug, much less to buy the place."

"This place makes four hundred and twenty five dollars every month, on the average, and Mr. Pettigrew has agreed to take a half interest for what I owe him. Which is just a hair over two thousand. You can take my other half for a two thousand dollar note. Between you and I and those batwing doors, I have a little savings stuck away so I can get a new start in California. Don't mention it to Mr. Pettigrew, as he'd like to think of me groveling on the streets of San Francisco." For the first time she looks a little angry, then continues, "You pay me two hundred a month for one year and that will include some interest. All you've got to do is run her right and the Angel will pay for herself. And you can still take wages just as you have been . . . Mr. Pettigrew has agreed to that."

I stare at her for a long moment. Then say quietly, "You and Mr. Pettigrew must have had it out once and for all. I can't condone a man who would strike a woman, nor could I be a partner with one . . . no matter how good the terms."

She smiles at me, rather sadly, then offers, "In a few months you could go to St. Louis and get a fancy new limb for that leg of yours."

"You don't suppose Mr. Pettigrew would take the same deal and sell me his half?"

She laughs aloud and shakes her head. "Mr. Boone, you are looking a gift horse in the mouth. If I were you I'd be dancing a jig right now at this opportunity."

Again, I give her a long look, then nod. "I'm sure you're right, but I want to talk to Mr. Pettigrew first. The God's honest truth is I don't want a partner." I glance around to make sure no one can overhear, then speak in a lower tone. "You and I both know what Mr. Pettigrew is capable of, and partners are trouble enough."

She smiles, this time sincerely. "Mr. Pettigrew thinks the world of you, Mr. Boone."

"And I him, with certain reservations. I still need to talk with him before I can give you an answer."

"Fine."

I rise, and start to leave, then have second thoughts and turn back. "You sure I could make the payment?"

Again, she laughs low. "If you make sure Horace doesn't steal more than that dollar a day he puts in his pocket, and that the dealers don't as well, and that the girls report what they get over and above the half dollar you pay them for every token they turn in, you'll do fine. I won't lie to you, Beau, this is a hard business and it takes a hard soul to run it. Everyone will think they're entitled to more than they honestly earn. Handle that, and the Angel will take good care of you."

"And Mr. Pettigrew doesn't want to run the place."

"He's got bigger fish to fry. He'll be watching over your shoulder, you can be sure of that."

I nod, shrug, and head for my stool. I'll wait for Mr. Pettigrew to show up before I make up my mind. Even a gift horse might well bite.

It's an hour before Mr. Pettigrew arrives, and walks right on by Miss Alice without speaking, and she keeps her eyes glued to her journals as he does so. It must have been quite a night at the cottage.

He comes straight to me. And I fight laughing out loud, as his shiner is bigger than the one Miss Alice has. She gave better than she got. In fact he looks as if he's been hit with her flat iron.

"Well, Boone, are we partners or not?"

Again the bard comes to mind: "Neither a borrower nor a lender be; For loan oft loses both itself and friend, and borrowing dulls the edge of husbandry."

# CHAPTER TWENTY-TWO

"My father, before he was burned up along with my ma and two sisters when the Union fired our plantation, always told me that Shakespere's most important advice was 'neither a borrower nor a lender be.' "

Mr. Pettigrew smiled at that, a rather condescending smile, then offered, "So, you're gonna let three hundred year old advice run, or should I say ruin, your life?"

"I think it's sound today as it was then. But I am willing to forego that advice on one condition."

He's looking down his nose at me as if he's questioning my good sense. He shakes his head. "You're a damn fool, Boone, you don't take the deal Miss Alice offered."

"It's not Miss Alice's deal, it's yours, Mr. Pettigrew. I don't like partners, much as I've come to admire much about you."

"So, you won't take her deal?"

"No, sir, I won't. However, if you think

buying into the Angel with what's owed you is a good deal —"

"The deal stinks, except I get the hell rid of the whore —"

"Don't call her that, please. She's been a fine lady to me."

"The deal still stinks. I would never pay that much for half the place if it wasn't for the fact she's headed out of town."

"Then if you don't think it's worth that, how about I overpay you. I'll give you a note on the same terms for the two thousand she owes you, and you walk away."

"Hell, Wilkenson will kill you and you'll never get it paid."

"Then what kind of a deal will you take?"

"Cash money, and it's two thousand two hundred sixty five dollars."

"I don't have that kind of money," I say, with a shrug.

"Then I guess Miss Alice and I are still partners. Come see me when you have the money."

"That will take me a while at two dollars a day."

"Then I guess it'll take you a while. Tell whoever asks that I'm going over to the Olympic for a decent breakfast."

Again, I shrug, as I'm sure Miss Alice can hear all that's been said, but she doesn't look up as Mr. Pettigrew passes and pushes his way out the batwings.

She rises and walks over after he's gone, and brings me a cup of coffee. I get a pat on the shoulder as she climbs up on the stool next to me. "You made a wise decision, Beau. He's no one to partner up with, and to tell you the truth I felt bad after I suggested it. I can't fault you for turning me down."

"I have yet to turn you down, Miss Alice. But I need to figure a way without having to watch my back all the time. I might consider a partner, but not Mr. Pettigrew as much as I admire much about him."

"Like I said, I can't fault you."

Friday night is surprisingly quiet, the tables with only a couple of players, and only three stools at the bar occupied, and them with Hutchinson, the hostler where my gelding is stabled; Andy McBride, the barber; and Doc Stony Peabody. The only strangers in the place are a couple of drummers from Salt Lake City, one peddling farm implements, one patent medicine.

In fact, I've never seen the place so slow on a Friday night. Maybe Miss Alice knows something about declining business that I don't? Hell, I'm getting paranoid as a saloon operator, and I'm not yet close to becoming one.

For the first time since I arrived in Nemesis I'm hoping tomorrow night, Saturday night, will be as slow . . . but Andy McBride has already informed me that the Dead Horse Canyon mine is back in full operation, losing only two miners in the cave-in. We can expect a full contingent of miners, guards, and management in town to whoop and holler and probably shoot Mr. Pettigrew and I full of enough holes to make a decent sieve. The good news is the word's out that the mine is looking for another dozen employees, the bad . . . they are probably being hired on as killers, not miners.

Why should I worry about making a deal on the Angel when, odds are, I won't live long enough to agree and shake hands.

Saturday night proves to start out with a house full by six p.m. At least three dozen customers are at the faro tables, the roulette wheel, and taking trips out to the cribs with Blossom and Martha Ann, but by eight o'clock, by the Seth Thomas on the wall, the boys from the mine still have not arrived. I can only hope that Wilkenson has cooled down and accepted the fate of his sons . . . but I don't for a second believe it.

For the first time since I'd walked into the

bank to open a savings account, I see Simon Chastaine who comes in and goes directly to the bar. He does not cut his eyes my way, and I get the impression he is expecting to be thrown out, his business unwanted, as I was from his establishment. Were it my place, that's exactly what would happen.

Mr. Pettigrew is at his normal place in the front corner away from the bar, his back to the wall, his coach gun leaning in the corner. He's working his normal three fingers of whiskey, but nursing it slowly, which suits me as the night is young and my backbone is getting stiff . . . there's a fight on the wind, I can feel it.

I realize that men are slowly filtering out of the saloon, and where there were three dozen or more, we're down to about a dozen and a half. I can see that Mr. Pettigrew is cutting his eyes around, watching closely as if he, too, thinks something amiss.

Chastaine has been moving around the room, talking with the locals. Still they leave. I realize then that everyone remaining in the place is someone I don't know. The drummers are still here, but there's another ten, in a variety of dress — drovers, freighters, farmers — who must be from out of the area or passing through on the train and laying over. It makes me suddenly anxious and suspicious.

Then Chastaine, for the first time, meets my gaze. He tips his bowler, and he too, exits the place.

I had envisioned the threat coming from those in the bar, none of whom I know, but then the batwings push aside, and in walk four burly men, each carrying a scattergun.

Pettigrew is on his feet, double barrel sawed off coach gun in hand.

With surprising ease, I vault the bar with my scattergun in one hand and the second on the bar, up against the wall.

Horace, wisely, finds a reason to drop behind the bar and re-arrange the items on the shelf there. Horace calls to me from his hideout, "Dead Horse guards."

The four mine guards space themselves out across the front of the bar, two of them facing Mr. Pettigrew, two of them facing my way. In seconds the remaining patrons and the dealers, Aleandro and Porter, sense the trouble coming, and half hit the front doors and half the back. Blossom follows those out the back; Martha Ann must already be there with a customer.

Now only Miss Alice, who's put her back to the wall near the rear door; Horace the bartender, who's crouching behind the bar; Mr. Pettigrew, his back to the wall, his revolver palmed in one hand and the scattergun in the other; and myself, my revolver still holstered but a double barrel sawed off in each hand, remain.

Things then begin to happen as if in slow motion. As my eyes are glued to the two guards facing me, from over fifteen paces away, I don't see Caleb Wilkenson step through the back door, a Golden Boy Winchester in hand, until it fires. Mr. Pettigrew has his attention fully on the two guards facing him, and never sees Wilkenson until the heavy bullet smashes into his chest, blowing him back against the wall, his double barrel, probably merely a reaction, fires both barrels, and both guards facing him are blown off their feet to their backs.

I spin to face the new threat, Wilkenson, who's jacking in another shell, but I'm late. Miss Alice, from only two paces, has raised a small belly gun and it discharges. Wilkenson stumbles my way, but goes down in a heap after three steps.

Knowing I'm too late, and likely dead, I spin back to face the two guards who've had their sights on me, but luckily over half of me is sheltered by the bar, and to my surprise, Horace has thrown a heavy beer mug, bouncing it off the head of one of the mine guards, and distracting the other momentarily, but it's enough.

He's trying to bring his muzzles back to bear on me, and almost does as one barrel spits fire and barrels smoke my way, but it splatters into the front of the bar. My neck's on fire; but with purpose I fire both barrels of one scattergun at one of the guards, folding him in the middle. The other's got a hand on his bleeding head while trying to focus on me, and I fire both barrels from the other scattergun. The first is blown back through the batwing doors, arms windmilling; the second through the multi-paned window on the bar side of the doors, smashing it and landing on his back on the boardwalk outside amid a thousand shards.

I've never heard such silence, abbreviated by my heart beating in my ears, by the ringing of my ears, and by the dryness in my mouth. I raise my hand to my neck and realize I've taken a shot or half-a-dime or a piece of square nail, whatever the load was, across the side of my neck. My hand comes away covered with blood. I feel the spot again, and although there's a wound, it's not pumping blood.

The only movement in the room seems to be the swaying of a chandelier, and the gentle wafting of dust motes filtering through the gunsmoke.

Placing both scatterguns on the bar, I hoist the converted Army 44 revolver in the holster at my waist, just to make sure it's riding free and easy, and let my gaze try to penetrate the smoke in the room.

Miss Alice, eyes wide staring at her handiwork on the floor, her bottom lip between her teeth, has her back to the wall, the belly gun still in hand hanging limply at her side. Wilkenson, his eyes and mouth open, staring at whatever he sees in hell, is in a fetal position on the floor, gray matter and blood seeping from the exit wound in his head. He looks very surprised, if a dead man can.

The front half of the saloon is covered by blood and gore from the four men who've taken loads from three scatterguns, Mr. Pettigrew's and my two.

At that I vault the bar again, and move as quickly as peg and leg will take me, to where Mr. Pettigrew is on his back, blood flowing from mouth and nose, breath raspy, pink lung blood oozing from the hole in his chest.

I get there in time for him to give me a grin, then a wink, then a gasp and a death rattle, then silence.

To my great surprise, it looks as if I'll make that Sunday picnic tomorrow, if I can get the bleeding in my neck stopped.

Holding one hand against the wound in my neck, I gimp my way back to Miss Alice and take the gun out of her hand. "You better have a seat," I suggest, and lead her to a chair at one of the faro tables.

Horace is on his feet, eyes wide, scanning the room. His mouth is hanging open, which is appropriate considering the scene.

Slowly, Doc Peabody pushes through the batwings, and looks around as if he doesn't know where to start, and to be truthful, it doesn't matter. I'm the only one on my feet. Only then do I realize I've taken a chunk of shot in my left shoulder as well as the wound in my neck. A couple of other locals follow him in, then, to my surprise, Jessie Traintor runs into the saloon, her eyes covering the room until they meet mine, then she hurries to my side. Ripping a scarf from her head she pushes me into a chair at the same table as where Miss Alice is still wide eyed, and goes to work on the wound in my neck.

"Didn't get an artery," she says, to herself more than me, "but it'll take a few stitches. In and out clean. You are a lucky man, Beau Boone."

"Lucky to have you looking out for me," I say.

"You stay. The doc will get to you in a

minute. I'm going to see if I can help him, then I'll be right back."

"Is Azzelea dead?" Miss Alice asks.

"Who?" I reply.

"Azzelea. Mr. Pettigrew."

"That's his real name, Azze . . . whatever."

"That is his name, much as he hates it. Is he dead?"

"Yes, ma'am."

"Then it'll be A. Pettigrew on his headstone."

I'm a little surprised at her quick acceptance of his demise.

She continues, "Then our deal is done. You owe me four thousand at four hundred a month, as I can now sell you his share as well."

"Can't do it," I say, my voice more firm than I feel.

She pauses, surprised, then inquires, "You won't have a partner, and Wilkenson is a dead man," she says.

"Make it two hundred a month for two years."

She comes close to a smile, which is a little bit of a surprise under the circumstances, her paramour lying dead across the room. Then she extends her hand and we shake.

Jessie returns to my side and works to bind the wound in my neck, then pulls away my shirt when she realizes I've got a wound in my shoulder. "You're going to be laid up again."

"No, ma'am, you're not getting out of that picnic that easy. I can drive a buggy one handed if necessary."

Horace walks over and inspects the job Jessie is doing on my wounds.

"Horace," I snap at him.

"Beau," he replies.

" 'Above all to thine own self be true.' Advice from the bard and I. You've been tapping the till for at least a dollar a day. I'm the new boss here, and I'm giving you a dollar a day raise."

He grins.

"But if you touch one damn penny that doesn't belong to you, I'll take your leg off, maybe both legs off, at the knee, understand?"

He looks sheepish, but nods.

Jessie stops her ministrations long enough to place a hand on Horace's shoulder and add, " 'And it must follow, as the night the day, thou canst not them be false to any man.' "

"Yes, ma'am," Horace says, but he's looking a little confused.

"Thank you, Horace," I add.

He's looking even more confused.

So I explain, "For the mug. Damn good throw. Damn good."

He smiles widely.

It's nice to be appreciated.

Now, if only the remaining Wilkenson sons, one with a scar on his chest, one minus a forearm, are content with owning papa's gold mine.

Somehow, being Wilkensons, I doubt it.

# ABOUT THE AUTHOR

**L. J. Martin** is the author of over three dozen works of both fiction and non-fiction from Bantam, Avon, Pinnacle and his own Wolfpack Publishing. He lives in, and loves, Montana with his wife, NYT bestselling romantic suspense author Kat Martin. He's been a horse wrangler, cook as both avocation and vocation, volunteer firefighter, real estate broker, general contractor, appraiser, disaster evaluator for FEMA, and traveled a good part of the world, some in his own ketch. A hunter, fisherman, photographer, cook, father and grandfather, he's been car and plane wrecked, visited a number of jusgados and a road camp, and survived cancer twice. He carries a bail-enforcement, bounty hunter, shield. He knows about what he writes about, and tries to write about what he knows.

The employees of Thorndike Press hope you have enjoyed this Large Print book. All our Thorndike, Wheeler, and Kennebec Large Print titles are designed for easy reading, and all our books are made to last. Other Thorndike Press Large Print books are available at your library, through selected bookstores, or directly from us.

For information about titles, please call:
(800) 223-1244

or visit our website at:
gale.com/thorndike

To share your comments, please write:
Publisher
Thorndike Press
10 Water St., Suite 310
Waterville, ME 04901